A Cairndhu Nightingale

&

Other Tales

Jim Shields

Cover Design by Brittany Wilson | Brittwilsonart.com
from original paintings by Ulster artist, Cherie Craig |
https://www.cheriecraigart.com/

In memory of our son, Paul Fergus Shields

And grandson, Lewis Patrick Shields McCartney.

It is said time succours loss.

We mourn until we meet again.

Children

You are our conception,
We waited for you
To leave the mother womb.
We nursed you through infancy,
Nourished you through childhood,
Guided your adolescence,
Saw you grow.

Mentored you to maturity,
Fuelled your imagination,
Rejoiced in your being,
Gave you wings to fly.

Freed you to go solo,
Anywhere your imagination knew.
All hopes and aspirations
Fulfilled in you.

Table of Contents:

A Cairndhu Nightingale

The year is 1956. Billy MacBride will celebrate his birthday in October.

On a Sunday afternoon in August, the front door of a mid-terrace house on Meetinghouse Street eased open. The front wheel of a bicycle nosed its way out onto the doorstep. A young man, one hand on the handlebars, the other grasping the saddle, bumbled the bicycle down three steps onto the pavement. With a flick of his foot, he released the kickstand and parked the bike at the kerb.

It was a sturdy machine with a substantial, well-sprung saddle, rod-operated brakes and a parcel rack fitted over the rear wheel on which Billy had tied a brown paper bag containing a bunch of flowers.

Billy MacBride bounded back up the steps, closed the front door, locked it, secured his trouser bottoms with bicycle clips, athletically mounted the bike and cycled away down the empty street.

Morning service in the Unitarian church across the thoroughfare that gave the street its name had ended. Worshippers had gone home. The road was quiet.

Billy turned left onto Pound Street, cycled along Victoria Road, and left again onto Glenarm Road and then onto the Coast Road.

He was going to visit his mother in 'The Sir Thomas and Lady Edith Dixon Hospital' in Cairndhu.

The youngest of four children, a bachelor, Billy lived with his mother after lung cancer had taken his father to an early grave. His father, a lorry driver, often took Billy with him, transporting merchandise around the country, chain-smoking one Woodbine after another, window open as he drove. Smoking was fashionable then. Billy loved sitting beside his father up-front in the big lorry. He felt important, proud, and grown-up.

Few understood the dangers, then, associated with passive smoking. Billy's mother, a non–smoker, was diagnosed with lung cancer some years after his father passed.

After surgery to remove one-third of her lungs, his mother was transferred to 'The Sir Thomas and Lady Dixon Hospital' in Cairndhu to convalesce. Billy was all the family she had close at hand. His siblings lived abroad.

Sitting straight-backed on the bicycle, Billy leisurely peddled into a refreshing north-easterly breeze. It wasn't far to the hospital. He could have walked, but cycling, he was through the Black Arch and Drains Bay in no time.

Looking over the sparkling sea towards the Mull of Kintyre, he noticed the little granite stone-built boathouse nestling under the branches of the tall trees, unaware that a previous owner of Cairndhu House used it when sailing from Scotland to his summer residence.

Rounding a bend, he was suddenly at the hospital entrance. Dismounting to get his bearings, he felt corralled by head-high curved granite stone walls, linking the wide sandstone-pillared entry at the roadside to matching sandstone pillars set further back from the road.

Pushing his bicycle slowly across the entrance apron between the inner pillars, Billy proceeded unchallenged past the small granite-stone-built gatehouse. Above the gatehouse door was a sandstone plaque set into the masonry, but he gave it little attention.

The avenue wound steeply upwards through columns of tall trees and shrubs rich in summer foliage. Billy recognised oak, elm and Scots Pine, and the trees seemed to get taller as he walked up the avenue. It was quiet except for the all-around birdsong. The trees hedging the pathway on both sides formed an arched canopy, creating a micro-climate underneath. After peddling in the bright sunshine along the Coast Road, Billy appreciated the dappled shading and the cooler air. He felt secluded, safe and secure on a journey of discovery, wondering what it must have been like to have lived in a place like this.

Idly pondering, Billy thought he had reached the end of his trek, only to discover that the avenue veered off to the right as another path branched to the left. Had he gone left, he would have passed the walled garden and the chalet known as Carnfunnock House. Billy stayed on the tarmacadamed path as it wound onwards and upwards.

Leaning on his bike, pushing it along, the tall trees and shrubs hedging the avenue on his left became less dense, inviting his curious eyes and mind to search beyond.

Suddenly, it seemed to Billy everything around him quietened; the birds were silent. He tensed; his hands tightened their grip on the bike's handlebars. Every nerve in his body was alert. He stopped and stood rigidly still, listening to the surrounding silence.

"Are you going to the hospital?" A voice behind him asked.

Turning to look, Billy's hands tightened further on the handlebars of his bike. A young woman, dressed from head to toe in white, stood in the middle of the avenue, smiling at him. Bemused, he stared at her. She wore a white cap on her head, a white dress and a white apron. Her dress collars and cuffs were broad and stiff. White low-heeled shoes covered her dainty feet. Billy searched for his voice as the young woman stood smiling at him. It was like she was in her natural habitat, part of the landscape. Her hands were empty. She carried no bag, no purse, and was without accessories. The above-average height, slight figure, with a free and easy way of walking, moved closer to Billy. Rooted to the spot, he was unable to move.

Her voice had a little lilt that commanded his attention, "Did you hear me? I asked if you were going to the hospital."

"Yes. I heard you," Billy managed to say. "Sorry, you startled me. I thought I was alone."

"Oh, I didn't mean to startle you. I'm on my way back to the hospital. I always take a walk around the walled garden at lunchtime. I saw you passing; you seemed unsure of…"

"I'm going to visit my mother in the hospital. I've never been here before, you see."

"I'll walk with you if you don't mind."

"My mother was transferred here yesterday. It's my first chance to see her. I'm a bit anxious about her you see, she's had a big operation," Billy stammered. He could feel his neck colouring.

"Your mother is fine. There's nothing to be anxious about. It's time I was getting back to work anyway," the young woman said as they continued up the avenue to the hospital.

Names exchanged, it never occurred to Billy how his companion, Florence, knew about him and his mother. The avenue Billy noticed sprouted little secluded paths, some edged with strips of flower beds, leading invitingly to where he knew not. Seeing his curiosity, Florence explained that they led to different features: summer houses, arboretums, arches with all sorts of climbing plants and seating areas.

As they walked, she pointed out trees thought to be 150 years old, many of them 75 feet and more in height.

"Sir Thomas Dixon bought his wife Edith's childhood summer residence, Cairndhu House and the land that went with it, later acquiring Carnfunnock, substantially increasing his estate;" Florence said. "This was a lively place when the Dixon's lived here, you know. They entertained a lot and hosted many house and garden parties. They employed over 20 house staff and 30 gardeners and estate workers." Delight coloured her voice. In her telling, it was as if she had, somehow, been part of it.

In full flow, Florence explained that Cairndhu House was a War Hospital Supply Depot in World War II, hundreds of soldiers recuperated in Carnfunnock, and German prisoners of war worked there too.

Speaking with conviction and affection for the place, she explained that to celebrate his 79th birthday, Sir Thomas gifted Cairndhu House and a substantial chunk of his estate to the Ministry of Health and Local Government for use as a convalescent hospital. To maintain their association with Cairndhu, they built a chalet bungalow, Carnfunnock House, beside the walled garden.

Pausing in the middle of the avenue, her brief history of Cairndhu House finished, Florence, looking Billy in the eyes, said, "That's where we're going now. It's just around the bend."

The hedging of tall trees and shrubs on Billy's left gave way to chest-high-trimmed hedging as they rounded the bend in the avenue, leaving clear, unobstructed views of The Sir Thomas and Lady Edith Dixon Hospital that had opened in 1950, the first convalescent hospital in the estate of the Northern Ireland Hospitals' Authority.

Gazing up at Cairndhu House, Billy let his eyes drift slowly down over the terraced gardens, level by level, to reach the avenue where they stood. Slowly reversing the process, he raised his eyes, searching the terraced gardens, one by one, until Cairndhu House, set against the backdrop of Sallagh Braes, filled his eyes. In amazement, he stared at the array of pointed roofs angled skywards, the vast windows, and the glossy ivy covering the facade. *People lived, entertained, and had house and garden parties here. It must have been a sight to see,* Billy thought. *It's breathtaking.*

Moving closer, he counted the steeply angled pitched roofs that projected out from the front of the house with their ornate pierced fascia boards adorning bow windows. To Billy's inexpert eye, no two windows were the same. Some windows opened onto an ornate balustraded balcony that extended almost the length of the house, creating a veranda underneath, paved with limestone slabs, onto which French doors allowed access. Plants freely climbed around the columns supporting the balcony, adding colour and fragrance to the porch and patio. Billy momentarily thought he could detect the sweet smell of Jasmine but couldn't be sure as he had only been introduced to it once before. Green, yellow and orange coloured ivy clinging to the facade caught his eye too, as he looked up again at the scattering of chimneys topped with eye-catching handmade clay pots piercing the slated roofs.

Parting at the massive hardwood door at the entrance to the hospital, Florence showed Billy where to go, took her leave, and went cheerily about her business with her easy way of walking. Billy watched until she disappeared out of sight. The sun, casting shadows over the immaculate lawn in front of the veranda, led his eyes down through the terraced gardens. It was a breathtaking, elegant, manufactured landscape.

Making his way tentatively through the high-ceilinged entrance lobby to reception, a porter directed him to the visitors' lounge where his mother would be waiting. Billy would discover that all the rooms in the hospital had high ceilings.

Approaching the lounge, he heard music. At the open doors, he paused; patients and visitors were seated in a semicircle, facing a troupe of young dancers dressed in traditional costumes enthusiastically dancing their jigs and reels. Sitting alone at the edge of the semicircle, Billy's mother was furthest away from him. She didn't see him. His mother disguised it well if she felt out of it because he was a little late. Lifting a chair, Billy tiptoed over and sat just behind her. Her hand beat time, with the taped music and her feet itched to dance. Engrossed in watching the Metson School of Irish Dancing perform their reels, jigs, and hornpipes, she was unaware Billy had joined her. The performance, lasting more than an hour, ended in rapturous applause. He would learn from his mother that it was something the dancers from the Metson School often did for the hospital.

"I think you enjoyed that, Mother," Billy whispered.

Turning to look at him, she said, "Auch, Billy, it's you, son. When did you get here?"

"I've been here a wee while. You were enjoying the dancing so much I didn't want to spoil it on you."

"Away with you, Billy. It brings back memories, I can tell you, son. A taste of that for breakfast would do anybody the world of good. But wasn't it great? Don't you think? How are you doing, Billy?"

"More to the point, Mother, how are you doing?"

"Auch, Billy son, I think with entertainment like that and the good grub, I'll be able to suffer the next six weeks all right," she answered, laughing.

On the veranda, they strolled up and down, Billy, brown paper bag in one hand, the other one supporting his mother, taking in the view. They had the veranda to themselves. The blending scent from the climbers rooted in the cast iron planters was intoxicating. Sensing his mother needing to rest, they took the lift to her room on the second floor.

His mother shared a spacious, airy room with five other women with access to the balcony. On one side, two beds sat on either side of a marble fireplace. Three beds filled the other side. His mother's bed, beside the access to the balcony, had an excellent view of the gardens. With his mother resting, Billy found a vase for his flowers. He thought, looking down on the terraced gardens in full bloom, his small bunch of flowers didn't look like much, insignificant in fact, but the view in the afternoon sunlight, framed against the purple hues of the Scottish hills in the distance, was spectacular.

"You'll have to up your game, Billy son," he told himself as snippets of Kipling's poem *'The Glory of the Garden'* flitted across his mind:

'a garden that is full of stately views,
Of borders, beds and shrubberies and, lawns and avenues.
With statues on the terraces and peacocks strutting by;
But the glory of the garden lies in more than meets the eye.
Oh, Adam was a gardener, and God who made him sees
That half a proper gardener's work is done upon his knees,
So when your work is finished, you can wash your hands and pray
For the glory of the garden that it may not pass away!'

Billy didn't see peacocks; but he spotted cock pheasants and heard their raucous chatter.

With Kipling's words vividly illuminating the humanity of the garden, turning to his mother fumbling in the brown paper bag,

Billy extracted a bag of her favourite toffees: rhubarb and custard bonbons, and sheepishly set it on her bedside cabinet.

Smiling, his mother said, "Auch, Billy son, you shouldn't have bothered; you're an angel."

They chatted until the tolling bell signalled visiting time was over. Tentatively, Billy moved the conversation to visiting for the week ahead; weekday visiting was difficult for him. His mother, her mind as sharp as a tack, was way ahead of her son.

"Next week will look after itself, son. Don't be worrying about me. If you can't content yourself in a place like this, there must be something wrong with you."

"Are you sure, Mother? I don't want you sitting on your own when visitors surround other people."

"I told you not to worry about me. There are not so many visitors during the week anyway. You look after your job, son. I'll be looking forward to seeing you on Saturday. Okay?"

"But…"

"No buts, Billy," she said laughing. "For once, do what I tell you. There's plenty here to keep me busy pottering around in the gardens and the library. If I want anything, wee nurse Florence looks after me, the best you've ever seen. She's a wee angel that one; looks in to see me every night."

"Florence?"

"Yes, Florence. She might have popped in while you were here to say hello."

Content that his mild-mannered mother was happy in herself, Billy said, "See you on Saturday then," and left as the tea trolley appeared.

Carefree, he freewheeled down onto the Coast Road and went home.

The days seemed to fly past. But at night, he slept fitfully. His subconscious played scenarios around his mother's recovery.

Angels, cherubim's, seraphim and thrones in joyous chorus circling above his mother as she lay in bed, celebrating her recovery or welcoming her into Paradise? The tangled knitting in his subconscious mind climaxing with bands of trumpeting angels forcing him awake night after night, awaiting the knock on the door telling him she had passed.

It was gone 10 a.m. on Saturday when Billy eased himself out of bed and raised the window blind to let the new day in. He was anxious. He had things to do before setting off to visit his mother.

It looks the way I feel, Billy thought. It was one of those benign, overcast summer days, neither too hot nor too cool. The dull and lifeless sea did little to help his disposition. An attaché case replaced the brown paper bag on the parcel rack on his bike.

Pushing his bike up the avenue to the hospital, Billy met Florence again as she exited the path from the walled garden, uniformed as a nurse, as she was when they first met. Surprised but not disappointed, Billy brightened and greeted her cheerfully, "We meet again."

"Yes, indeed we do," she responded, glancing at the attaché case.

"I thought I should bring my mother some… ah, ah, personal things, her wee necessities," Billy apologetically proffered by way of explanation.

Smiling, Florence changed the conversation, "Your mother's doing really well. You'll see a big difference in her."

It was very welcome news for Billy, considering the nightmares he'd had. He thought about mentioning them to Florence but couldn't persuade himself to.

As they walked, Florence entertained him with stories about what Cairndhu House was like in former times. Where the trees and natural shrubs merged with maintained hedging, Billy paused again to allow his sensory faculties to fully absorb and appreciate the beauty of the terraced gardens, stepping up and plateauing into lawns towards the majestic ivy-mantled house.

Florence, sensing his rapture in a calm voice, said, "It's fantastic. Isn't it?"

Billy looked at her and nodded.

At the hospital entrance, they again went their separate ways. In the visitors' lounge, Billy found his mother seated with patients and visitors in a semicircle, listening to music and people singing. The sound pouring out of the lounge filled the hospital with joyful notes. It was uplifting. Sitting beside his mother, Billy enjoyed Larne Choral Society's entertainment; everyone was encouraged to participate in the merry-making, and some patients, including his mother, didn't need much encouragement. Patients and visitors heartily contributed. The room vibrated with energy and well-being.

It was evident to Billy how much his mother enjoyed the afternoons' entertainment. The improvement in her from last week, too, was noticeable. *At this rate, she'll be out of here much sooner than she thinks or might want. Who would want to leave this?* Billy thought.

In her room, setting the attaché case on her bed, he unfastened the clasps and left his mother to unpack her necessities. Billy had included things he knew she liked but didn't ask for.

Finished unpacking, she turned, smiling a mother's smile said, "Thank you, son, that's great. Let's go for a wee walk around the gardens."

They walked and talked the rest of the afternoon away. Without a window box or a flower pot in her enclosed dreary yard, his mother confidently named plants as they walked. *All this in a week,* Billy thought, *she'll want a greenhouse when she's back home.*

All too soon, it was time for visitors to say their farewells. Billy dallied as long as he could, but in the end, he reluctantly had to leave. "I don't think you'll need me to fetch you anything tomorrow. Will you, Mother?"

"No, son, not a thing. If I need anything, I'll ask Florence; she'll be doing her rounds tonight. God love her; she's a wee angel, that one."

Florence again, Billy thought, as he pushed hard on the peddles for home; *she must work different shifts.*

Sunday dawned bright, sunny and cheerful. Billy, with a good night's sleep behind him, happy in himself, set about the household chores, cooked an early dinner for one and set off on cue to see his mother.

On his way up the avenue, he met Florence again – the third time – accepting it for what was – fate. Billy asked Florence where she lived and why she wanted to be a nurse. And more.

Florence, in return, revealed that in times past, her family lived in the area and that she had always wanted to be a nurse, caring for people. She told him she was part of a small in-house team providing night cover and other duties when needed.

Florence advised Billy that his mother's recovery had been so good that she might be discharged sooner than anticipated.

Billy was conflicted. He knew it was good news, but did he really want to take his mother away from all this back to their little whitewashed house on Meetinghouse Street? He knew his feelings didn't matter; he had no choice.

Florence, sensing his anguish, comforted him, saying, "Don't worry, Billy, your mother will be fine."

With her assurance filling his head, Billy went to find his mother. She wasn't in the visitor's lounge. Her room was empty. He searched the library, but she wasn't there either. Frustrated, he walked out onto the veranda to discover his mother at a distance down the gardens, frantically waving and rushing towards him.

Embracing him, she apologised for her tardiness. "I'm sorry, Billy, I went for a walk and lost track of time. This truly is a wonderful place. There is so much to see and enjoy. Come, I'll show you," she said, taking his arm and leading him along.

Concerned for her well-being, Billy reluctantly followed her lead. His mother seemed to have a reservoir of boundless energy, much more than he had. They explored arm in arm for nearly two hours as they toured the grounds and gardens. Billy didn't need any convincing that his mother's discharge from the hospital was, as Florence said, imminent.

Leaving, Billy stopped on the avenue and, straddling the bike, looked back at his mother framed in the centre of the veranda and felt her inner beauty radiating to him. He waved one-handed, and she responded with two.

Work filled Billy's days. Angels, including Florence, happily dancing filled his dreams. Suddenly, it was Saturday. Billy, care-free, easy in himself, on his way to see his mother, cycled along singing to no one in particular.

He met Florence again. *Four times, in the same place, at the same time. It can't be a coincidence,* he thought, *can it? Could it be she likes me a lot? Why not? There's nothing wrong with me. Is there? I like her a lot, I think?* All sorts of interrogating thoughts wrestled around in his mind. It was the first time Billy had felt the faintest touch of Cupid's arrow. He didn't know what to say when Florence asked him what he was thinking.

Searching for his mother, he found her in the visitor's lounge. She was seated straight-backed, her posture good as always in the semi-circular arrangement as before, listening to members of Larne Drama Circle reading a play. Joining her, Billy settled to listen. Patrick Byrne's play, 'Lord Tyrone and Lady Beresford,' was an excellent pick for a reading as it explored a tragic event in his Lordship's residence and was well received by an appreciative audience.

When they retired to his mother's room, she whispered, "They're sending me home tomorrow, Billy."

"Great mother, how do you know?" Billy asked, sensing a hint of regret in her voice."

"Florence told me last night to be prepared. Doctor Wilson, on his rounds this morning, told me himself."

"Did they say what time or anything?"

"I think you'll need to ask the matron, son, before you leave today."

"I will, and I'll get a taxi to take you home in style. How's that?"

Visiting time at an end, Billy went to see the matron. She ushered him to her office, setting him down, offering refreshments, which Billy declined. The matron had almost finished updating him on his mother's health and the necessary domiciliary care she assumed he would provide when she noticed him taking an interest in the silver-framed photograph sitting proudly on her desk.

"That's my daughter," she said, "she's a nurse too."

"It's a lovely photograph. She has your likeness."

"It was taken on her first day on the ward after qualifying as a nurse. I'm very proud of her," she continued, turning the frame towards Billy for a better look.

"Does she work here?"

"No, why do you ask?" There was a hint of wariness in her voice.

"Oh, it's just that I met someone like her."

The matron, pursing her lips in thought, asked, "Someone like my daughter?"

"Yes."

"Where did you meet her?"

"I met her here. A nurse who lives and works here, you must know her. She was very attentive to my mother, looking in on her every night."

"What's her name? Do you know?"

"Florence."

"You've met Florence?"

"Yes."

"Did she tell you anything about herself?"

"Not much, No."

Without going into too much detail, the matron told Billy about the tragic death of a young girl in Cairndhu House many years ago. Her parents were entertaining guests on New Year's Eve. The child, in a white nightdress, crept out of her bedroom on the top floor to view the gathering below. Standing up, she leant too far over the railing and fell into the middle of the people below. Death was instantaneous. Her name was Florence. The ward Billy's mother occupied was Florence's room.

"Oh, I didn't…"

"Florence must be very fond of your mother and you," the matron continued.

"My mother always said she was an angel," was all Billy could offer back.

"Well, then Billy," Matron said, bringing their chat to an end, "I suggest you collect your mother after lunch tomorrow if that's okay with you. It will give her time to say her goodbyes and let you both get away before the visitors arrive."

***

The year is 1966. His mother's health a cause for concern; Billy made what alterations he could to their home on Meetinghouse Street to address her increasing infirmity. Afraid of the narrow winding stair, he made a bedroom downstairs. But more disruption and upheaval were to follow. Billy and his mother were rehoused when their neighbourhood was redeveloped in 1970.

She celebrated her eightieth birthday the year they returned to Meetinghouse Street to live in a purpose-built retirement unit. Back where they belonged, Billy and his mother were delighted.

In 1986, the same year that 'The Sir Thomas and Lady Edith Dixon Hospital' closed, Billy's mother died. Billy sat with her alone through her passing.

In one of her lucid moments, she asked, "Billy, can you see her son?"

"Who, Mother?"

"My wee guardian angel. Florence?"

"Yes, Mother, I can see her," Billy, white, lied.

"She's never left me, Billy; she'll take care of you too, son."

Those were her last words. Billy hadn't seen Florence, but he felt her presence with his mother at her passing. She was in the room with them.

From her first day in the hospital, his mother had called Florence, her wee angel, without knowing the whole story. He recalled the matron's words; "Florence must be very fond of your mother and you."

When Carnfunnock Country Park opened as a tourist attraction in 1990, Billy was among the first through its gates; his destination was Cairndhu House. He took a little while to orientate himself and find the avenue leading up to the house. It was overgrown and neglected. Standing where he had before, with unobstructed views from the bottom of the terraced gardens up to the big house, he blinked and reset. Now, he looked through

overgrown shrubs. Closing his eyes, he hoped that what he saw
was just a figment of his imagination. But it was not. A jungle of
brambles and other undesirables shrouded the terraced gardens.
The magnificent house was in ruins. It pained his eyes to look at
it. Kipling's words reverberated around in his head;
So when your work is finished, you can wash your hands and pray
For the glory of the garden that it may not pass away!'
And the Glory of the Garden it shall never pass away!

Billy's heart possessed the glory of Cairndhu House and its gardens forever. It would pass away with him and others who
appreciated their glory.

For many years, Billy went to Carnfunock Country Park
every weekend to visit the remnants of Cairndhu House. It was
his weekly pilgrimage, but he never saw Florence again. Neither
did he meet or hear of anyone claiming to have seen Florence.
But on his visits, Billy felt her presence close by his side. He
often paused on the avenue, waiting, hoping to hear her asking
again, "Are you going to the hospital?"

Ghost hunters have often visited Cairndhu House. But Billy
and his mother are the only people known to have seen and spoken to Florence, The Cairndhu Nightingale.

Dancing with a Painted Lady

Morning in the garden
Weeding flower beds.
Soul cleansing
Exacting but necessary.
Lord have mercy.

The risen sun
Warming my back.
Birds noisily foraging
Chorusing encouragement
The garden is alive.

Resting on a bench
Eyes sun shielded,
Coffee in hand
Thoughts idling
Contentedly I sit.

A flicker of movement
Invites my errant eye.
What is it?
Snuggling in the grass
Barely discernible.
A translucent flutter
Rainbows of colour

Flooding my imagination
Unfolding wings
Disclosing a migrant.

Moving in rhythm
With the fluid grasses
Mosaic of mottled colours
Red brown white
Yellow and orange.

On spidery legs
She poses before
Deftly dancing on
Spear pointed
Bladed grass.

Pirouetting she pauses
Attracting my eye with
Her invitation to dance.
Moving closer closer
Whispering her solicitation.

We dance together
On the green carpet
Soaring high higher
Diving deep deeper
Spinning in our imaginations.

In a whirlpool
Of purest pleasure
We float together

Strangers in that moment
That is life.

The dancing ends
Goodbyes exchanged
She flutters away.
My heart goes with her,
Utterly happy am I.

Rise Above It

Alighting from the train, Cedric leisurely made his way up Station Road. It was a beautiful September Saturday morning. His purpose in town was twofold: to visit his mother and watch the home team, Larne, playing in the Legion, or what was now called, Inver Park. He considered it a duty to see his mother often; his siblings living abroad visited infrequently. At the top of Station Road, the football ground was only a stone's throw away, straight ahead, past Saint Cedma's Church. But he turned right over the bridge and took a left up Mill Street.

The Old Town was Cedric's playground; he was familiar with its streets, lanes and alleyways. Walking from the station, Cedric wandered at ease through old childhood haunts. He arranged visits with his mother to coincide with Larne's home games, the afternoon kickoff time giving him a plausible reason to end his visit. Up Mill Street, he took a left onto Ferre's Lane and then a right onto the Knowe. With his back to the three little white-washed cottages strung across the top of the Knowe, Cedric looked down the length of the narrow gauge railway line winding its way out of sight around a bend. Beside it, the Inver River slowly gurgled its way towards the sea.

Across the river, the Legion football pitch waited, prepared for the match. Cedric's mind flooded with happy memories. So often he had captained his school football team there and represented his County, too. It was his field of dreams.

Leaving the Knowe and his reservoir of happy memories behind, he crossed the Ballymena Road to Kitchener's Avenue and turned right into Church Lane. Taking a left, passing more whitewashed cottages, he walked through Magill's haggard and up their backfield, through his childhood playground to the gate at the top that gave access to the Mill Brae. Pausing, leaning his back against the gate, he wistfully gazed over the panoramic view of the Old Town, the harbour, Islandmagee, Larne Lough and Inver Braes that he had not appreciated as a child.

Drawn back to the Legion football pitch, the scene released a treasured memory. Cedric was ten years old. On a Wednesday afternoon, his school played the Bridge School in the Schools' Cup Final. The match, a serious affair, was fast and furious. Supporters of both teams, hugging the touchlines, including some mothers, shouted encouragement as the teams came onto the pitch. When the final whistle blew, Cedric, the proud captain of the winning team, was presented with the cup and his winner's medal. There was a lot of celebration. After the match, when all the hullaballoo had subsided, Cedric joyfully ran home as fast as he could, his medal wildly swinging across his chest to tell his mother the good news. Hurrying in through the front door, dropping everything, he found her out in the yard, hanging out a string of washing.

"Mammy, Mammy. We won. We won the cup!" he shouted.

"Well done, Cedric, that's great," she replied, wrestling a wet blanket onto the line.

She was reaching for another garment when Cedric, tugging at her apron, said, "Look, Mammy. Look! Mammy, look, I got a medal."

She stooped to look at him and said, "Let me see it, son."

Beaming with delight, Cedric presented her his medal.

"That's great, Cedric. Now go and show it to Mrs Robinson, next door. She'd love to see it," she said offhandedly, handing Cedric back his newly won medal.

Confused, Cedric wondered if he had done something wrong. His bubble of enthusiasm burst, he took the treasured medal and trudged next door.

Mrs Robinson, an elderly lady, cradled his medal in her hand and showered Cedric with praise. Then, sitting him down, she listened attentively as he told her about the match and how proud he was as captain, getting the big cup and a medal. When he'd finished, she opened her purse, took out a thruppenny bit and handed it to Cedric, saying, "Here, son, that's for you. Well done. You deserve it."

Back home, he put the thruppenny bit into his money box. He didn't mention it to his mother. His mother didn't ask about his visit with Mrs Robinson.

That night, Cedric suppressed the sound of his distress as best he could, crying into his pillow. In his childish eyes, Mrs Robinson next door was more appreciative of his achievement than his mother. His mother wasn't on the touchline shouting encouragement. His father was absent, too.

"I hate her, I hate her. She doesn't love me," he repeatedly told himself, until sleep, nature's sedative, the balm of hurt minds, as Shakespeare put it, knitted up his ravelled sleeve of care.

He thought, *that was long ago. My siblings were too young to remember the Cup Final day.* But Cedric did—it still hurt.

A few steps from the gate, he was at the top of the Mill Brae, minutes from his mother's house. At the front door, he paused and surveyed the daunting 'Brae' that he had, at breakneck speed, sleighed down so many times. He pondered, *I don't think I would let my children sleigh down it.* Suddenly, he felt like a stranger looking in on himself, distanced from the people he had grown up with. *Or was that distance always there, and I was too young to recognize it?* He wondered. It didn't matter to Cedric. All that was in the past, and he had no desire to return to it. His future back then was to follow his father into the foundry, become a patternmaker, and work there for the rest of his life.

"A good, secure, steady job, son," his mother would say. Shaking his head at the thought, Cedric realized he lacked ambition then, content to take every day as it came; he wasn't looking ahead, didn't want to be anything and didn't know what to do with his life. He was drifting. *All that changed when I met Isobel,* he thought, thanking God.

Facing the door, he took a deep breath, knocked three times as he always did when announcing his presence and entered the house wondering, *how will my encounter with Mother unfold this time?*

His mother, a blow-in from up the country, as she was often referred to by friends, had come to Larne on the prevailing winds of opportunity at nineteen years old, searching for employment. Three years later, she married and set up a home in the house she still lived in - where she delivered Cedric. In addition to being tagged a blow-in, she was labelled a turncoat.

His mother brought her country ways to town, and as the firstborn of six children, Cedric was on the receiving end of her rural approach to parenting. He didn't love his mother, at least not as he thought he should. He just couldn't and wondered why. After much soul searching, Cedric's perception was that she had unwittingly, in rearing him, smothered his capacity to love.

Growing up, as her first child, he felt like a chattel, a dogsbody, a get me this, and a do that, a servant boy about the farm. It was her brusque manner, he would come to understand, that sowed the seeds of estrangement. She couldn't help it; the warp and weft of her upbringing had shaped her. When he reflected on visits to his maternal grandparents, Cedric was convinced that his mother was poorly schooled in the art of parenting. But as his siblings came along, his mother's parenting skills matured, so much so that the youngest, his brother Ian, many would say, was spoiled. Some might say, petted. Cedric often thought, *I would have welcomed some attention; I did the heavy lifting*, recalling again winning the cup and getting a medal. *No wonder*, he thought, *I felt resentful.*

Stepping into the small entrance hall, he opened the glazed inner door and let himself into the familiar front room. His mother, a long-widowed octogenarian, yet still facially attractive, was sitting with a cup of tea clasped in her arthritic hands, watching the television. Noticing her hands shaking, they hadn't shaken before, he wondered if his visit had induced it.

Banal courtesies exchanged, Cedric doffed his coat and set about ticking the boxes on the checklist in his head. Her fridge was well stocked - box ticked, kitchen neat and tidy - box ticked, gas controls as they should be - box ticked. He went through every room in the house and the backyard, ticking the boxes to ensure his mother was safe and secure, living independently in her own home. Satisfied that everything was as it should be, Cedric settled beside his mother on the chaise longue and helped himself to tea. Television permitting, they would chat about nothing in particular, tiptoeing like ballet dancers around the things that needed saying but were never said. They were like old sparring partners, going through the motions. Turning away from the flickering screen, his mother looked up at him, beaming a motherly smile. Cedric looked into her probing green eyes, momentarily wondering what she was searching for in him before disengaging and looking away.

She was talking about something; Cedric, losing interest, let his eyes wander around the familiar front room. Nothing had changed. The same pictures hung on the walls, the mahogany cabinet; her pride and joy in the recess on the other side of the Devon fireplace glistened in the fading light. The drop leaf table by the window where she sat Isobel when he brought her home to meet his mother for the first time was still there.

His eyes lingered there for a long time. Cedric well remembered that occasion. His mother, hesitant, uncertain and distant at first, was captivated by Isobel's openness and joyful personality. So much so that when parting, they were entirely at ease with each other, chatting freely like friends of long standing.

The silence grabbed Cedric's attention; his mother had stopped talking. Turning to face her, he saw she was slumped back on the longue, fast asleep.

Cedric wanted to whisper, "Mother, I do love you, have always loved you and will always love you, but I couldn't." He tried to lever out the words; his lips moved, but nothing left the prison of his encrusted heart.

They didn't have a television when he was a child; he remembered watching something at a friend's house. They were fortunate to have electric lighting. *Did we even have a wireless?* He wondered. His mother cooked the family meals on a primus stove; his friends' mothers had four-ringed gas cookers. The jaw box in the scullery was fed cold water through lead pipes, and the lavatory down the yard was stocked with neatly cut squares of newspaper, that served as toilet paper, pinned on a nail in the whitewashed wall. He recalled that little was wasted. It seemed his family was poor compared to some of his friends. Their poverty shamed the young Cedric. The good old days? Not in Cedric's experience.

Before he was ten, Cedric was the designated keeper of his mother's chickens, ducks and anything else she could rear that would earn an extra penny or two. He would fill and hump bags filled with discarded cabbage leaves and other suitable green stuff from Rab Mehaffey's greengrocers shop at the foot of Carson Street back home to feed his mother's growing poultry menagerie. Cedric did the same job from the allotments up the Lower Cairncastle Road, getting tagged with nicknames by friends making fun of him. In his childish eyes, it was a process of daily humiliation. He felt like a two-legged donkey or some other beast of burden in the public square.

Too young to understand that his mother had to use her country nous to make extra money, bitterness festered. But there was purpose in her endeavours. She sold fresh eggs and pullets and hens past their egg-laying days, out the front door to neighbours. Needs must and all hands to the wheel, but all that was beyond Cedric's comprehension then.

There was more. By age twelve, Cedric was a familiar sight in every pub in the town, searching for his father on a Friday evening to bring him home before he squandered his hard-earned wages on hangers-on. The Friday evening pub crawls made Cedric feel grubby and shamed. He knew nothing about alcoholism, but his festering resentment towards his mother and father intensified with each pub crawl. "She made me do it," he told himself repeatedly, loading more blame onto his mother without realising it was all borne out of necessity.

Fast forwarding a few years, everyone had a credit card, expediting transactions remotely without embarrassment. Still, at his mother's bidding, Cedric had to stand in the grocer's shop asking for credit, whilst neighbours' ears cocked, listening. It didn't matter that others were doing the same. What mattered to him was that his friends weren't doing it.

One incident scarred Cedric physically and emotionally. He had been on one of his mother's chores, but being the boy he was, he took time out with his friends to play football on the nearby college green. Time passed quickly. Cedric didn't notice as he was enjoying himself. Then his mother appeared furiously waving a leather belt. Cedric froze as his infuriated mother ran towards him, wildly swinging the belt. She had come looking for Cedric, armed. She had a temper, and her intentions were clear.

Raging, she grasped the belt's tail, freeing the buckle end. Cedric was hit with a fierce blow just above his left eye, knocking him to the ground. The next thing he remembered was waking up in the doctor's surgery feeling dizzy, with the wound above his eye stitched and dressed and fit to go home. *How did my mother explain the wound above my eye to the doctor?* Cedric often wondered.

There wasn't a definable Damascene moment in Cedric's search for the truth. Firstborn, an impressionable child, fed on the gruel of his mother's country rearing; his subconscious suffered. In adolescence, he would embark on a bumbling journey of self-discovery. He began collating and dissecting what he thought he knew. His realities.

His mother adjusting her position on the longue attracted his attention. She was still asleep. As the thoughts swirled around in his head, it occurred to him that his mother might harbour regrets about his upbringing that nagged her, too. Lost in thought, he heard his mother addressing him.

"Did you come back after the match, Cedric?"

He had to gather himself before responding.

"I didn't go, Mother. You were asleep. I didn't want to wake you."

"You should have gone on. Sure you like the football. I remember the day we got you your first pair of proper football boots. I'd be alright, son. I can take care of myself, you know. You should have gone to the match."

Cedric had forgotten about getting the new football boots and wearing them the day they won the cup. *She remembers the boots,* he thought, *but not winning the cup and me getting a medal.* Shrugging, he said, "Well, I'll need to be going now, mother. Isobel will be wondering what's happened to me."

"Give Isobel my love, son."

"I will, Mother." With that, Cedric leaned across, patted his mother on the hand, flesh on flesh, given, taken and returned and took his leave.

It had taken Cedric a long time to travel this far on his journey of self-discovery, but the further he travelled, the more he became the son he wanted to be. He was learning to unlearn feelings that were long past their sell-by date.

On the train, Cedric randomly rummaged through his fragmented memories. As a child, he had lots of freedom: playing football on the street, creating adventures in the surrounding fields, long Sunday walks past Mc Kelvey's little sweet shop on the way to the standing stone at Killyglen and the annual trek to the nut braes, at Craiginorne. *My children don't have that kind of freedom,* he thought.

He had joined with pals in collecting anything that would burn for the July bonfire at the foot of the Mill Brae. It was fun. His mother didn't stop him from doing it; even if after a day's foraging, she had to wash his clothes on a scrubbing board and hang them out to dry down the yard.

The fun ended when he was twelve. With pals, he went over to the factory end of the town on bonfire night. It was part of the tour they did around the bonfires every year. On this occasion, a girl Cedric recognized from college pointed at him and addressed his pals, "What's he doing here?"

No one answered her.

At first, Cedric was non-plussed. Then, it dawned on him that he wasn't welcome. He was somehow different. Cedric never helped with the bonfires again. If his mother noticed, she never mentioned it.

He often heard her say to her children, "There are some things you must learn for yourselves, or you'll learn the hard way."

Years later, reading Seamus Heaney's poem, Clearances, the tag turncoat pinned on his mother came to mind,

A cobble thrown a hundred years ago
Keeps coming at me, the first stone
Aimed at a great-grandmother's turncoat brow.
The pony jerks and the riot's on.
She's crouched low in the trap
Running the gauntlet that first Sunday
Down the brae to Mass at a panicked gallop.

His mother never mentioned if she had to run the gauntlet to Mass; Cedric often wondered what it was like being branded a turncoat.

His eldest child arrived home from school one day with an assignment to develop an outline of her family tree using the research methods discussed in class. She enlisted her father as her researcher. Curious, Cedric tackled the task with enthusiasm.

At one point he had his parent's marriage certificate lying on the table, with the children's birth certificates, scattered around it. Cedric focused on his birth certificate. He stared at it, occasionally glancing at his parent's marriage certificate. Something compelled him to stare, to search. But for what? Then he saw it. It was the dates right in front of him in plain sight, in black and white. He was illegitimate, conceived out of wedlock. Cedric sat momentarily numbed, staring at the documents, absorbing the import of his discovery.

His daughter, bouncing into the room, asked, "Find anything interesting, Dad?"

It forced him into the moment's reality. Cedric certainly had things to think about; how he had shielded his pent-up feelings of resentment towards his mother, categorized them, shut them away, stored them up, letting a bitter crust cover his heart. *Now this*, he thought selfishly, *more stuff to bury* before centering his thoughts on his mother.

What was it like for her? When did she tell her family? How did they react? Did they want to put her away? Have her child adopted? Did his father accept his responsibilities? An avalanche of questions streamed through his mind. He, Cedric, was the answer to all his questions. Conceived in love, he entered the world with a birth certificate to prove his legitimacy and, importantly, his parents' fidelity.

When the house had quietened, Cedric told Isobel what he had discovered.

Isobel, smiling, asked, "You're not bothered about being conceived out of wedlock. Are you Cedric?"

"No, I'm legitimate. Don't I have a birth certificate to prove it?" He retorted, smiling, tongue in cheek.

"You know what I mean."

"It doesn't bother me; I have my life to live. We're all inclined to be a bit too judgemental, I think."

"Isn't that what you've been doing, judging, concerning your mother?"

"Perhaps."

"Will you tell our children about your discovery?"

"Yes, if I have to. Why not? I've nothing to be ashamed of."

"Good. Maybe your mother feels she has nothing to be ashamed of, too. She'll have regrets, I'm sure. We all have. In the crucible of home, Cedric, there's lots of love, patience, tolerance and gratitude. But often intolerance, ingratitude and impatience surface. Look at us; we have our moments, we're not perfect. Our children sometimes don't like doing what we ask them to do. Your mother's life wasn't easy, far from it. She may have temporarily lost something of her feminine gloss. Your mother loves you very much, Cedric. You are, after all, her love child. Hold that thought in your heart."

Continuing, she said, "From the first day I met your mother, she opened her heart to me and couldn't do enough for us ever since. Do you know what I think, Cedric? It was her oblique way of telling you she thinks the world of you."

"You think so?"

"Absolutely; your mother has given everything she had to her family. She couldn't have given more. Your father, a Monday-to-Friday angel, was a weekend burden she could have done without. You appreciate that. Don't you?"

Cedric, nodding in agreement and smiling, said, "I thought she cared more about her chickens than me."

"But lots of things were going on in your mother's life that you didn't know then. Your brothers and sisters will have different memories and perspectives on growing up, just as you do. Their collected perspectives would present an incomplete picture of her. You can see that. Can't you? Add your father's and others' perspectives into the mix, and an enhanced collage of your mother's personality would emerge, but it would still be incomplete. Add in my mine too, and there would be gaps, gaping gaps and no doubt distortions, but personalities formed in the eyes of beholders, imperfect perhaps, are nonetheless valid to them."

"I know how you feel about my mother, Isobel; you've told me often enough. I appreciate it, and you've helped me a lot. Thank you."

"I'll never forget the first time I met her. I couldn't have been made more welcome. She showers her love on our children, and they adore her. We're all on a learning curve, Cedric; look at how far you've come."

"It has been a journey, Isobel," Cedric quietly acknowledged.

A virtuous silence descended on Cedric and Isobel as he cogitated and pondered on everything he wanted to say but couldn't say to his mother. To bare his feelings, blaming her for all the unhappiness in his childhood was still a mountain too high.

"I tried," he told himself.

"You didn't try hard enough," his alter ego challenged.

Mentally, he debated with himself.

Isobel, ever the pragmatist seeking a way forward, broke the silence, saying, "Look, why don't we pay a surprise visit to your mother tomorrow afternoon and take her out to tea somewhere."

"Why?" Cedric responded.

"Why? To tell her how you feel about her. You almost told her today. Another little step, and you're there. You have been building empathy for your mother in all your soul-searching. I think you realize that you are not the only one feeling regretful. We all do one way or another."

"You feel regretful."

"Yes, of course. Many things I could have done differently and better. It's all part of the journey we are on."

"But, but…"

"No buts, no excuses. Think about your childhood and the freedom to go out and play on the street with your chums. You had more freedom than our children have."

"It's a different world, Isobel."

"Of course it is. Things change; that's why you're revisiting the past, to free yourself of some of it."

"Look, there's no doubt that I see my childhood in a very different light. But..."

"I said no buts. You are a good person, Cedric. You need to know that. Why do you visit your mother so often? Your siblings living abroad are your excuse to hide behind duty. You do it because you love her. But it would help if you acknowledge your feelings to your mother, who has to reciprocate. Then we can all look forward."

At five past three on Sunday afternoon, Cedric parked his car outside his mother's house. Isobel, first out of the vehicle, knocked three times on the hall door and breezed into the empty front room.

"Hi, Lily, it's only us popping in to see..."

Aromas of home baking seeping from the kitchen and filling the front room made Isobel pause and smile.

Cedric's mother, popped her head out of the kitchen as Cedric joined Isobel; taken by surprise, she apologetically said, "Oh, sorry, I'm just finishing up in here. Sit down, I'll be with you shortly."

She joined them in less than a minute, insisting they sit down and share what she had just baked.

Lily purposefully raised the drop leaf of the widow table into position, covering it with a crisp white tablecloth from the mahogany sideboard and rearranged the matching chairs as she had done so many times in the past for them.

Watching his mother, it struck Cedric forcefully that there was something sacramental about what she was doing. Something that mothers do daily and is taken for granted.

Lily served the tea in her best china, with homemade wheaten and soda bread, lashings of butter, blackberry jam and cheddar cheese. Satisfied with her table, she ushered Isobel and Cedric to their seats. When all three were seated they tucked in and chatted. Lily, as always, asked about their children. Isobel enquired about Lily's health, and so the conversation continued. Cedric was somewhat reticent.

Isobel, sensing the tension building in him, wondered if his mother could feel it, too.

When the conversation lulled, Lily excused herself and headed into the kitchen, returning with a home-baked apple tart.

"Would you like a decent piece or a small slice?" she asked Isobel.

Served with vanilla ice cream, it was delicious.

After the tea, Isobel insisted that she clear the table, load the dishwasher and tidy up so that Lily could rest and talk to Cedric. She closed the kitchen door, leaving Cedric and his mother in an uneasy silence. Behind the door, Isobel listened momentarily before turning her attention to the kitchen.

Cedric, searching for words of acknowledgement, looked up as his mother turned from the mahogany cabinet behind her, holding a small battered tin box. Setting it on the table, Cedric got a closer look. It looked like an old, well-used lunch box. There was nothing fancy about it.

"Something I want to give you, son," she said, looking Cedric in the eye. "I've held onto it for too long."

Slowly, she prised off the box lid and extracted a folded newspaper cutting. With trembling fingers, she unfolded the cutting, turned it around to face Cedric and slowly eased it across the table to him.

Cedric stared at the photograph of himself lifting the cup in the Legion, twenty-five years ago.

"I'd forgotten all about that," he unconvincingly said before continuing, choking up on the words, "It was a long time ago, Mother."

"It was, son, a long time ago, but you don't forget a day like that. Do you? It was a great day, a happy day for me, Cedric. I've often taken it out and looked at it. I am very proud of you, son."

Cedric, sitting transfixed, like a rabbit caught in a car's headlights, didn't know how to respond or what to say; he thought, *she's kept this cutting all these years, hoarded like an heirloom.*

His mother, reached into the tin box and extracted a soft leather pouch. Loosening the drawstring, she let the contents fall out close to Cedric, saying, "I'm sorry, son. I've kept your medal too long. It's yours. You must have it, show it to your children, tell them all about it, please."

"Why, Mother?"

"Why? It's yours, son."

"Mother, why did you keep my medal and the cutting?"

"I wanted you close to me, Cedric. That's why."

Cedric, reaching out across the table, took his mother's arthritic hands in his, flesh on flesh, given, taken, forever bonded.

His Journey

Where to begin?
Begin at the beginning.
It began innocently
Summer sighing its passing
Young lovers on a mossy bank
Mantled by a beguiling moon
Consummate their fidelity.

Love a vigorous
Fragrant evergreen shrub
Flourishing in soil
Emotionally enriched
Affectionately husbanded
Gifts itself
In any season.

Spring came late
He arrived early
Bursting out of darkness
Thrusting into newness.
A new beginning in
The continuum of being
That is living.

Granny's Grit

Early morning, standing on the crest of the Mill Brae, the sun rising over Islandmagee, Sean gazed with unblinking eyes at the townscape spread out before him. In the crisp, clear early April morning, his osprey eyes zeroed in on familiar places: the Town Park, the vacant spots on the promenade where bathing stations used to be, the Carnegie Library, his old school, the 'Legion' where he played his football and the Inver River where he learned to swim.

In the foreground, his mind's eye overlaid the Riverdale area, with the Old Town's network of lanes long swept away in its creation. The Knowe, Ferre's Lane, Black's Lane, Mission Lane, Cooper's Lane, Trow Lane, Hamilton's Row, Mill Race, Mill Lane and the factory with its red brick hexagonal chimney that had indiscriminately spewed out its odious polluting effluent; its stump standing out like a sore thumb. Momentarily pausing his hawkish scrutiny, he acknowledged the presence of the one remaining tower block of three, which also condemned, stood patiently awaiting the nudge of the demolition ball.

Poets and others had eulogistically penned words on paper lauding the old, disappeared ghetto and its inhabitants in wistful recollections and imaginings. Outsiders, looking in, remote voyeurs, distanced, detached from the reality of lane living. But Sean knew it for what it was; stripped of its nostalgic gloss, a warren of lanes, a slum. Did the spectators see the deadpan faces of the women and look into their expressionless eyes as they leant forward, backs bent as if walking into a stiff breeze, lugging a bag in each hand, on their daily grind, through the lanes?

Did they notice the young men, fathers, and grandfathers shabbily dressed, everything about them screaming poverty, hopelessness and deprivation, hosting corners, smoking fag ends. Others passed their time walking greyhounds or pigeon fancying. They had the same face set as the women folk, faces of resignation, proclaiming their drudgery.

The arterial life of the lanes flowed through Mill Street's shop-fronted premises with their extensive outhouses and well-maintained two and three-storey properties. Business people, merchants, doctors, writers and poets lived on Mill Street; their set faces drudge free.

Although socially distanced, it was a community of street and lane dwellers that were interdependent in many respects. Glad the slums were gone, he regretted the scattering of what was a close-knit community.

Beyond the factory chimney, his gaze settled on Mill Lane and the rubble stone, whitewashed end of the terrace house that was his humble home, where he began himself; it was familiar territory. Backing onto the narrow gauge railway that tracked alongside the Inver River, mumbling its way to the sea, Mill Lane wasn't much to look at unless you could give the scene some pastoral form with an artist's eye.

He could see the shiny metal pipe spanning the river that he and his friends shimmied across to sneak into Inver Park to watch Larne play their home football games. That was a fun thing to do. Children made their own mischief then, inventing games and creating magic while growing up, blissfully unaware of their parents' daily struggle.

There were no birthday celebration days in his home. It just wasn't the done thing, except at Christmas, when some foods not tasted from one year's end to the next were shared, when his mother's purse would allow. Fruit, an apple or an orange, usually filled his Christmas sock.

***

Outside by the railway, sitting on a stone, tying hooks on his fishing line, his grandmother, wrapped in a black mantle, slowly shuffled towards him like a waddling duck. Alerted by her dragging feet, he was surprised to see her approaching, as she seldom left her comfort by the turf fire. A few feet from him, she stopped, cocked her head and looked down at him with her good eye, as he'd seen chickens looking down into the neck of a bottle. Catching his eye, she paused, gathered the mantle closely around her scrawny shoulders, took a deep breath and resumed her shuffle.

Leaning on his shoulder, he felt the clutch of her gnarled fingers. He was big for his age and sturdy; she pushed a big red tin cylinder into his hand with her other hand. Sean didn't know what she was giving him but liked the colours on it. Nonplussed, fumbling it in his hands, trying to figure out her purpose, he heard something rattling inside. It was about twelve inches long and two inches in diameter, bright red with gold stars sprinkled all around it. One end had a kind of capping piece under which there was a slot. Sean thought it looked like the pillar box on Pound Street people put letters in, the one he passed every day on his way to school.

His granny, reading the confusion on his face smiled her toothless smile and said, "You don't know what it is, son?"

She always called him son. He liked that. It made him feel something of worth to her.

"No, Granny. It looks like a pillar box you put letters in."

"Well, Sean, it's for putting something in, right enough, but not letters."

"What'd I put in it, Granny?"

"Money, Sean, it's a money box, son, for saving your money in."

"It's not a box, Granny. I don't have any money."

"Sean, it's called a money box because when you have money, you can save it for something you want to buy. You could save up to get yourself something you want for Christmas."

"What'd you mean, Granny?"

"You put money in the box, when you have it, save it until the money box is full, then you empty it, and start all over again and keep on doing it until you have gathered up a lot of money."

"How do you get the money out, Granny?"

"I'll tell you that when you've filled the money box, son."

Slowly cottoning on to the idea, he said, "Something's rattling in it."

"There is, son. I've put something in it to start you off saving. Saving is a good habit to cultivate. Let's see how long it takes to fill your money box, Sean. You don't always have to be poor, son, you know. Ok? You can make something of yourself if you want to. Rise above it and get yourself out of here, son."

With a wave of her bony hand, she shuffled back to her place by the fireside. Sean tried unsuccessfully to get the something out of the box before discarding it and returning to fixing hooks on his fishing line. Years later, he realised the red money box was his first birthday present.

Three weeks later, Sean, arriving home from school, wandered over to the kitchen table, expecting to find a piece of bread and jam. There wasn't any. Disappointed, he glanced over at his granny sitting by the fire. She was slumped in her chair, sleeping, and the fire was almost out. Setting his schoolbag aside, he put a few turves on the fire. Satisfied that the fire would return to life, he attended to his granny. She was very still and quiet. Usually, when sleeping, she would make noises, twitch, and turn. There was no twitching or turning. She was very still.

Puzzled, Sean spoke, "Granny. Granny, are you alright?"

There was no response. Sean gently shook her. She didn't respond, and she felt cold to his touch. He tucked her shawl around her and fetched a neighbour from next door.

His granny had died peacefully in her sleep by the fire.

It was Sean's first experience of death—a glimpse of his mortality. Sadness and confusion clouded his young mind, causing him to think that, had he been home a little earlier, she might not have died. Then, seeing her in the coffin, staring at her lifelessness, she looked so small, tiny and insignificant—a nothingness. Pangs of sorrow pierced his heart, and try as he might not to, he shed childish tears. With her, on his own, he bent over the rim of the coffin and kissed her goodbye. It was an experience he would forever remember.

A few days after Granny's funeral, in a box he kept odds and ends in, Sean found the red money box she had given him as a birthday present a few weeks before. Sitting on his bed, he pressed it to his heart and, fighting back the tears, remembered what she had said to him,

"You don't always have to be poor, son, you know. Ok? You can make something of yourself if you want to. Rise above it and get yourself out of here, son."

That was when he realised the purpose of the red money box she'd given him; saving his money was his ticket to a new life if he wanted it. It was also the moment Sean decided he wanted it very much. But it was easier said than done. He had to figure out a way to earn money before saving it. The family was living hand to mouth, his mother stretching every penny she had as far as she could make it go.

Sniffing around for a wee earner, Sean discovered that there was money in stuff people threw away, like jam jars. Retailers would refund the purchaser's deposit on returnable glass items like jam jars in good condition. So he sallied forth to build his future with earnings obtained harvesting jam jars. The Old Town, where every penny was a prisoner, was slim pickings for Sean. But he got to know the retailers and what they wanted. Ensuring his merchandise was first class, he became a trusted trader. Business was initially slow but improved as his widening catchment area included more affluent neighbourhoods. He scoured them for merchandise. Folk living there didn't need to reclaim their deposit on a jam jar. Sean gladly relieved them of that burden.

As his business grew, he included milk and Porter bottles in his returnable repertoire. In no time, he was familiar with and had returned bottles to every pub in the Old Town. He made a trolley with old pram wheels and onion boxes, which he converted into a small pull-along trailer to cope with increasing business.

Sean kept his money box in the glory hole, a makeshift cupboard underneath the stairs to the loft. When no one was around, he would get it out, deposit his week's earnings, feel the weight of it, and turn it upside down, trying to gauge how full it was. Christmas was coming, and in Sean, anticipation was growing.

His heart was set on a proper fishing rod. His rod was fashioned from bits and pieces he found, or friends had given him. Like his fellow fishermen, he just wanted a rod that looked right. Fishing rods were expensive; he frequently checked the prices in the local angling shop but would settle for an excellent second-hand rod if he hadn't the funds to buy a new one.

Sean, however, was conflicted. He also wanted to give his mother a Christmas present. She was always giving, putting herself last, but he wouldn't have enough cash for two purchases.

Christmas was fast approaching; the money box, almost full, had room for a few more coins. Sean kept a weekly tally and knew that he might, just might, have enough saved to buy a second-hand fishing rod, but he would have nothing left for a present for his mother. Another week will do it, he convinced himself.

The house was quiet. It was a Friday afternoon two weeks before Christmas. His mother was out doing her weekly shop, penny stretching as usual, and his father, he knew where he would be after work. With his weekly earnings pocketed, Sean eagerly went to the glory hole to retrieve the money box.

Kneeling, he gingerly opened the hatch and plunged his hand into the gloomy interior, expecting to find the money box where he had left it. He couldn't find it. Anxious, he bent down and stuck his head into the glory hole to look, but it was too dark to see anything. He needed light.

In the scullery, he found the torch his mother kept for emergencies and hurried back to the glory hole. He saw it with one sweep of the torch, but not standing upright as he had left it. The money box was lying flat on the floor. Relieved, Sean eagerly reached in and grabbed it. Yelping, he let it fall, dropped the torch and quickly withdrew his hand. Blood trickled down his fingers, dripping onto the floor. Recovering from the shock, Sean rushed to the scullery, washed the blood away, and found some disinfectant to clean the ragged wound on the palm of his hand, which fortunately wasn't too deep. He bandaged the wound tightly with a tea towel and hurried back to retrieve his money box.

This time, Sean proceeded with care. Carefully picking up the money box, instantly registering that it was much lighter than before, he took it out of the glory hole. It looked all right until he turned it over to look at the side with the slot for inserting the coins. It was unrecognisable. The side of the money box was stove in. To his mind, it was like a hobnailed booted elephant had deliberately stamped on it. The money box was empty; all his hard-earned savings were gone. Stolen.

Anger boiled inside him. He felt stunned, resentful, enraged, violated and confused in a dizzying whirlpool of blending emotions that lurched towards vengeance and retribution. Like a trapped wild cat in severe pain, he screamed a silent oath. Curses and oaths he'd heard others utter, not knowing their intent; nevertheless, their earthiness seeming appropriate, he vented loudly. Then he crumbled into a heap on the floor and wept; a bundle on the floor, his blood-stained bandaged hand outstretched, and the battered empty money box beside him.

That was the scene that greeted his mother when she came home. With a glance, she took it all in, knew what had happened and who the perpetrator was. Comforting Sean, she saw his wound, cleaned and rebandaged it, and, trying to mollify him, asked what he had been saving for.

Sean talked and told her what he was saving for and his dreams. She tried to explain to him that his father's problem was an addiction, an illness. Monday to Friday, he was excellent, but weekends were difficult. Sean, choking back the swear words bubbling in his throat to spare his mother, wasn't convinced; he was too young, but he would come to a better understanding later.

"Please don't give up on your dreams," his mother advised. "Start again; the thief will pay you back in his own way; I promise you that, son."

He thought *you're just like my granny, full of hope.*

Sean stubbornly started again; on Saturday morning, he was out early with his pull-along trailer doing his business. He didn't get another money box. Sean kept the old battered money box by his bed to bolster his resolve to better himself. Adversity, he had learned, could be a helpful teacher, too. The day before Christmas Eve, he counted his meagre savings and searched for a present for his mother.

After Christmas, Sean opened a savings account in the bank and expanded his business to include the lemonade bottles well-to-do folk jettisoned. Always looking for a way to earn an extra penny or two, he sought and obtained a much sought-after paper round for Phillips' paper shop on Pound Street. Sean was chuffed. He didn't make a lot, a few shillings a week, but as his granny would often say, "There's not many shillings in a pound, son."

Throughout his early schooling, Sean ran his business, saving his earnings and watching them slowly grow, safe and secure in his bank savings account.

Leaving school a month before his fourteenth birthday, he found employment as an apprentice joiner. He never forgot his first week's pay: seventeen shillings and sixpence. Sean ran home with his unopened pay packet that Friday evening and gave it to his mother; it seemed like a lot of money to Sean. His mother grateful, thanking him, said, "It's your first pay, son, you save it. I'm ok this week."

His granny's voice screamed in his ears, *"She lives from week to week, son, but you don't have to. Get yourself out of here."*

Sean saved most of his first week's pay, but his savings would soon be stressed. He had no joiner's tools, and the tools of his trade were expensive. With a full-time job, Sean needed to reconsider his business interests. He reluctantly relinquished his early morning paper round, and the other business he curtailed to weekends only.

For the first few months, Sean was a joiners' helper, mainly labouring, but he learned how to erect scaffolding, know the difference between the floor and ceiling joists, and brew builders' tea. But little by little, he engaged in real joinery work and began filling his tool bag. His granny's foresight came to his rescue via his savings account.

In the workshop, Sean enjoyed learning how to construct sets of stairs of different geometries and making the cuts on rafters to create geometrically complicated roofs, often wishing he'd paid more attention in school.

The old hands seemed to take it all in their stride. Sean watched and drank it all in; it was mesmerising. In his second year, his pay doubled, and he enrolled as a part-time student on a City and Guilds joinery course in the 'Big Tech' in Belfast.

Time seemed to fly by. Sean gave up all his business interests; he could make more money by jobbing and doing joinery work. He was nineteen when he completed his apprenticeship, and a year later, he gained his City and Guilds diploma with distinction.

He had just turned twenty when something happened that changed his life in a direction he could never have envisaged; it was one of those coincidences, connections, a friend of a friend of a friend kind of a thing. An acquaintance of his mother called at the house one day to share some news. The gist was that the terrace of rubble stone built whitewashed dwellings they lived in was coming on the market for sale, with sitting tenants having first refusal. His mother's friend stressed that it was an opportunity to be carefully considered.

Sean looked at his mother and saw pleading in her eyes; if she had the means, he was in no doubt about what she would do, but she hadn't and couldn't, and his father was a beaten docket as they say, leaving Sean the only one left standing. Sean thought hard and long about his mother's friend's news.

His mother thought he'd bought their house; Sean didn't tell her he'd bought the whole row with a bank loan.

Later, Sean became self-employed, renovating domestic properties. Initially, it was challenging, but he succeeded, prospered and very quickly paid back the money he had borrowed for his first venture into the property market.

Two years later, when he and his girlfriend decided to marry, Sean bought a prime site overlooking Ballygally and built their home on it. Unfortunately, his father's death cast a shadow on their wedding day.

Sean's business flourished; his four children grew up well-educated, exercising their professional talents in different parts of the world. None of them followed in their father's footsteps into the construction industry.

Sean sold his building business and settled into retirement, although he kept his hand in doing odd jobs for friends. He was surprised at how wealthy he had become because he never set out to be rich. It just seemed to happen stealthily, incrementally. *Granny would be proud,* he thought, smiling; *I filled my money box, and it didn't take long.*

Her words rang in his ears, *"You don't have to be always poor, son. You can make something of yourself if you want to. Rise above it and get yourself out of here, son."*

Another of his granny's mantras wormed in his thoughts, *"There is nothing worth having son unless you can give it away."*

Sean's problem was how to give it away and for what purpose. He wasn't a mega-rich philanthropist, so creating a foundation or building a new hospital wing was out of the question.

Alone with his thoughts at the top of the Brae, he stood calmly breathing in the terrain that shaped him, where it all began, in the whitewashed terraced house on Mill Lane. The morning quietened and stilled as Sean, in his mind, relived the watershed moment of his life.

He could see her shuffling towards him along the one granny-wide spoor like a dandelion pappus carried on the wind, her shadow trailing behind, on a mission. The seed she brought and planted in him was a legacy, the notion that he didn't have to live a life of drudgery; he could make a better life for himself. His future was in his hands. All he needed was a little nudge from an old woman—her gift and words of encouragement in any language.

For him, she had forsaken her chair by the fireside, and he, in his childish way, had loaned her minutes of his precious time. As he saw her now in that watershed moment, shuffling back to her fireside chair, regret lay heavy on his heart. Sean remembered the 'something' she'd put in the money box, the 'something' stolen from him. It didn't matter now; she had given much more.

What little he knew of his granny's life was harvested from fragments of conversations with his mother before dementia rendered her memory unreliable. Of one thing, Sean was sure: he would not be who he is and what he had become without his granny's nudge.

His granny, Maggie Hamill, was a grafter. Life was tough, but she topped it out; he was her legacy.

In memory of her, Sean established two Maggie Hamill Scholarships in Architecture and the Built Environment, available to mature Northern Irish students enrolled on a part-time undergraduate degree course in Northern Ireland.

Asked why part-time mature students. All Sean said was, "They'll need determination and grit like my granny had to succeed and a bit more. It's my acknowledgement of my granny and a nudge to them."

The morning had lengthened when he left the town behind on his way to Ballygally. The trees, shrubs and hedgerows winter wearied beckoned another summer. He didn't look back; a glance was enough to contemplate the future.

It Was Only a Game

Darkness shrouded the little tin shed snuggling in the corner of the field at the bottom of the Mill Brae. It made a cosy den for the neighbourhood juveniles. The band of ten met as arranged in the Cassie off Church Lane and went unobserved to the Mill Brae. Furtively, they threaded unscathed through the barbed wire fencing into the field. It was a well-rehearsed routine. Like a skulk of hunting foxes shielded by hedging, they stealthily, in single file, approached their den. Quietly withdrawing the bolt and opening the door, they entered, securing it shut behind them.

Crescent-shaped, they sat on bales of straw around a lighted Tilley lamp, eagerly waiting for the telling of their ghost stories to begin. Each had a ghost story to tell. The den brimmed with animated murmurings as the luminous Tilly lamp flame flicked shadows around their young, keen faces.

All Souls Day is a day of prayer and remembrance for all the faithful departed. On this night, churches in the town prayed that the souls of all the faithful departed would rest in peace. A sacred silence imbued the den as the first storyteller prepared to open the proceedings.

A voice from deep shadow spoke, "I will tell you the true story of something that happened close to where we are to-night."

The silence thickened as the youthful voice launched into the story.

Bobby and Alfie, best friends, just teenagers, met with pals as arranged outside Milford and Rodgers general store on Pound Street. It was a wet, windy Saturday afternoon, perfect for their indoor hide-and-seek game. Bobby, the chosen hare on this occasion, had five minutes to secret himself somewhere inside the animal feed store before the hounds, Alfie and pals, were slipped to hunt.

In former times, decades before the arrival of supermarkets blighted the Old Town, Milford and Rodgers general grocery and animal feed store on Pound Street served the needs of its inhabitants and the local farming community.

A massive wooden counter stretched the entire length of the grocery store. Men in deep-pocketed brown coats and women in white, knee-length cover-alls served customers from an array of floor-to-ceiling shelves, often directed by customers' pointing fingers.

In an era spared the affliction of pre-packaged purchases, tea and many other commodities were sold loose per pound. Some loose purchases were served in brown paper bags, and others neatly wrapped in brown paper or newspaper. Buttermilk was sold by the quart and paraffin oil by the gallon. Customers ordered cheese cut from slabs with a wire cheese cutter, and rashers cut from bacon sides readied on the slicer. Hams, cured beef and fowl dangled tantalizingly from overhead rails. Other meats were stored in a cold room with a fine mesh cover to ward off flies.

It was a busy place, with the noise of the cash drawers opening and closing constantly, echoing loudly around the premises. In addition to providing essential services, it was a much-used social hub.

The animal feed, stored separately from the grocery shop, mainly was bagged pig meal, cattle meal, and chicken mash, with stocks resupplied every Friday. The arrival of fresh supplies on Friday made Saturday afternoon an ideal time for the boys to play hide and seek. With new hiding places to discover or create, it was game on.

The allotted five minutes for Bobby to secure a hiding place seemed to flash past, but it dragged on for the restless hounds itching to hunt. Then the ten hounds, in five pairs, with Alfie leading, like sighthounds, sprinted in pursuit of their quarry. But the first hunt was fruitless.

The pairs separated, and individuals began searching slowly and methodically like bloodhounds seeking a scent.

Alfie walked slowly, ears cocked for any giveaway sound, eyes searching every nook and cranny, finger trailing around hessian bags of feedstuff, all his senses alert for anything signalling Bobby's nearness. But Bobby, leaving no scent, no trace, evaded discovery even though chasing hounds employed different search strategies. Bobby was secure in his hiding place.

The increasing irritation of the hunting hounds eventually drew attention to their endeavours. About an hour before the store closed, the men in brown coats from the grocery store unceremoniously chased the hounds from the premises.

Huddled together at the corner of Carson Street, they waited for their elusive hare to exit and join them. They waited and waited, and waited in vain. Bobby did not appear. At six o'clock, the store closed, and the staff left the premises, locking the main door and bolting the doors to the animal feed store. There was no sign of Bobby. The waiting hounds across the street were bemused. Eventually convinced that he must have gotten out some other way, they slowly peeled off and filtered away one by one.

Alfie, anxiously lingered, reluctant to leave without Bobby. It was so unlike him, a prankster, maybe, but this was different.

They were friends, best friends, inseparable folk said, like twins, joined at the hip; seldom was one seen without the other. The thought that Bobby might still be in the feed store flitted across Alfie's mind. He thought, *maybe he got out a back way and is playing games with me.* Crossing over onto Pound Street, searching, Alfie turned left down Mill Street, then left again into Blacks Lane, where the row of whitewashed houses backed onto Milford and Rodgers' property, hoping that somehow, Bobby had exited the store that way. But there was no sign of his friend. Deep in thought, he walked into Mission Lane and back to Pound Street. Heading back towards Milford and Rodgers, he wandered in and around the Smithy opposite Carson Street, just in case Bobby had exited there. *If he had, we would have seen him, he would have seen us, and we would have joined up,* Alfie reminded himself.

Reluctantly, Pound Street now deserted, Alfie, the last of the hounds to leave the scene, despondently made his way home.

"Where have you been?" His mother greeted him. "It's gone seven o'clock. I suppose you've been with Bobby larking about as usual? Wash your hands; your dinner's warming on the hearth. I don't know what I'm going to do with you, Alfie."

Silence his defensive shield, Alfie hid his misgivings.

Later that evening, Alfie's thoughts fermented around Bobby, the fun-loving, medal-winning Irish dancer, altar boy, and his best friend. *Should I go and see if Bobby's home?* He thought, when a timid knock on the front door settled the matter.

"Come in, Sarah," he heard his father say.

Alfie knew that it was Bobby's mother. Bobby was an only child; his father, a fisherman, was lost at sea when he was seven. Alfie called Sarah his 'second mother' because she treated him as she did her son, and she had a heart of gold.

"Alfie, come down here a minute, son," his father summoned.

With dread mounting in his heart, Alfie slowly descended the narrow, steep stair.

Bobby's petite, neat and precise mother stood bundled together like a little rag doll, hunched by the fire, head bowed, clutching at her coat as if shielding herself from adversity. A glance at her anguished face told Alfie all he needed to know. Bobby hadn't gone home. He was missing.

"Bobby didn't come home, Alfie; his mother's worried about him. What can you tell us, son?"

Alfie told his story about playing hide and seek in Milford and Rodger's feed store. The hounds searched for Bobby but couldn't find him. They searched again and again but didn't find Bobby. The men in brown coats chased them out of the feed store. The hounds ran as fast as they could, every hound for itself, but Bobby wasn't with them. They waited until the store closed. There was no sign of Bobby. We thought he must have gotten out some other way. We waited and waited. Thinking he must have gone home, we left.

Alfie didn't mention his qualms, hopefully lingering after his pals had left the scene and his futile search of Black's Lane and the Smithy on Pound Street.

But why didn't you, Alfie, check to see that he had come home? Was the question Bobby's mother's distressed face flung at him? *You're his best friend. Did you abandon him? He wouldn't have left you, would he?* Alfie felt the shadow of Bobby entering the room as she looked at him. He didn't need eyes to see it; in his heart, he felt it. It was a shadow that would stay with him.

It was late evening when Alfie's father informed the police that Bobby was missing. Keyholders opened the store, and the search for Bobby began in earnest. The police-led search party worked all through the night without success.

The search for Bobby recommenced at first light on Sunday morning. It was painstakingly thorough. The bags of feedstuff were moved from one location to another in search of undiscovered hideaways. The likelihood that Bobby was not there surfaced in the afternoon and gained credence.

On Monday morning, Milford and Rodgers opened for business as usual. The bags of feedstuff were examined before being trolleyed out to the farmers for collection, a process pursued for the rest of the week in the search for Bobby.

The search had widened to include the streets and lanes in the neighbourhood. The Old Town was alive with searchers. They searched garden sheds, backyards, roofs and attics, and anywhere someone could hide, like places where the boys re-enacted Robin Hood's adventures, the narrow gauge railway line and the culverted drains that were favourite ambush locations. They searched the banks of the Inver River, the swimming holes they used, all the way up to The Plumb beyond Kane's Foundry. There was no sign of Bobby; it was as if he had vanished; disappeared into thin air.

The search for Bobby widened. Days became weeks, and weeks became months, with the hope of finding Bobby fading.

Alfie searched with a guilty conscience. He knew in his heart that he had deserted his best friend, abandoned him, and given up on him. Bobby wouldn't have left without telling him. He would have somehow signalled his intent. Alfie knew he should have checked if Bobby had gone home and that had he, perhaps everything would have turned out differently. And he was duplicitous in his account of events. Saddened and depressed, feelings of unfaithfulness and helplessness fell on him like a collapsing gable wall.

Alfie's nights were sleepless. Grief crept over him like a smothering blanket. He sometimes cried in bed in the night.

Afraid, alone with his conscience, he needed the comfort of a light to sleep. As time passed, his misery increased, and his schoolwork suffered. Bobby's mother noticed.

"It's not your fault, Alfie," she said, meeting him after another futile search. "Don't blame yourself. There's no point. Look after yourself, son."

In no time, slow time, it seemed to Alfie a year had slipped silently away since the Saturday Bobby disappeared. Walking past Milford and Rodgers's store on the opposite side of the street one day, Alfie cast a furtive glance towards the open doors of the animal feed store. Slowing, he tried to understand what he thought he had seen.

Retracing his steps, he stood directly facing the animal feed store. Alfie peered inquisitively into its dark interior, seeing shapes his mind told him were piles of bagged feedstuff where he had played hide and seek. Making to leave, he saw a figure emerge from among the piles of bags. It couldn't be, could it? Bobby was smiling and solicitously beckoning him to join in a hide-and-seek game. Alfie, ignoring the traffic, raced across the street. He stopped at the animal feed store entrance, afraid to accept Bobby's challenge. He lingered at the entrance as farmers shouldering their purchases went about their business. Bobby did not reappear.

Alfie retreated and went home. He told nobody about his encounter with Bobby if that was what he thought it was. That night, he lay in the brightly lit, unhappy bedroom, unable to think or move, with waves of guilt battering him from every direction.

But others must have encountered the ghostly figure in Milford and Rodgers's animal feed store because word spread like wildfire that the feed store was haunted.

The passage of time yielded nothing in the search for Bobby. But the investigation continued, informed intermittently by responses to local and national appeals.

In the years after Bobby's disappearance, his mother began languishing. Her faith, by contrast, was strong. She walked to the chapel daily for morning mass, bombarding God with gut-wrenching petitions for her son Bobby. In her generosity, she included all the missing in her petitions. After mass, she remained as the chapel emptied, thumbing her beads, reciting her litanies, imploring the Holy Queen of Souls and Refuge of the Lost to bring them home. That's how she spent her days and nights—praying in communion with the saints.

With time, Alfie's acute pain of guilt yielded to a dull, monotonous, but insistent ache. It was long before he summoned the courage to tempt sleep without a light on. His recurring dream was of a ship drifting silently in a stormy sea with mountains of water blasting into it. The boat was rolling, swaying and pitching heavenwards before plunging back into the ominous sea.

There were other strange occurrences. One day, on a bus going home from school, with assignments to prepare for the next day, ghostly images of Bobby filled his mind. His head began to spin; he grabbed the armrest on his seat to stop himself from dropping into a bottomless well of emptiness. His knees were knocking together so hard he propped them firmly up against the seat in front, afraid that people would notice his discomfort. This sensation happened intermittently all the way home, scaring him. But Alfie held these happenings fast in his heart.

When Bobby's mother became mobility impaired, she occasionally approached Alfie for assistance. A regular task he undertook was to light candles for her in the chapel. She was particular about the candelabras to use; the one in front of the

Sacred Heart of Jesus statue and the one in front of the Virgin Mary statue. She was also precise about the days and times when Alfie would light the candles because, on the appointed days, she would at home continue petitioning God on behalf of Bobby and all the disappeared people in the world with the lighted candles in the chapel, symbolizing her fervent prayers.

It was something novel for Alfie at first. He hadn't paid much attention to the holy things in the chapel before: the altar, the stained glass windows, the Stations of the Cross, the statues and the candelabras. In time, they seemed to speak to him. Draw him in.

Alfie was in his cold bedroom. It was night. Rain splattered loudly against the window glass. The light was on. Slowly, the room warmed. Suddenly, it seemed that Bobby, who had disappeared five years ago, was in the room with him—a real, tangible presence. The sensation was electrifying. It was as authentic and startling as if Bobby had stretched out his arms to embrace a long-lost friend.

An overwhelming sense of shame flooded Alfie's being; he had failed to do what he should have done, raised the alarm when Bobby, his friend, was locked in Milford and Rogers's store that fateful Saturday all those years ago.

The next day was one of the days Alfie was tasked to light candles in the chapel for Bobby's mother. He did as requested but didn't leave the chapel immediately, as he usually did. Hesitantly, he chose another candle, lit it and placed it in the centre of the candelabra, then knelt at the altar rails and slowly recited the Lord's Prayer with all the belief he could muster. Alfie hadn't prayed much before. His sin of omission forced the impassioned prayers from his heart and tears from his eyes. Alfie left the chapel feeling unburdened. He'd done something that needed to be done. That was all he knew. His candle of atonement lighting his way.

In bed, that night, Alfie, feeling at peace with himself, switched the bedroom light off and held his breath. Nothing happened. It was the first time since the Saturday Bobby disappeared that he had dared face the darkness in his mind. Reciting a rosary of Our Fathers, he drifted into sleep.

How long he slept, he didn't know. Music played softly in his head, lullabies he had heard somewhere before. The music got louder in his ear, jigs and reels that Bobby had danced to. Suddenly, he awoke startled. The music stopped. On other nights, someone tap-danced to the music. It was loud. He knew it was Bobby making himself known. At breakfast, no one mentioned the loud music. Alfie let it pass.

A few nights later, a shuffling noise outside his bedroom door on the landing interrupted his sleep. It sounded like a cat, but they didn't have one, or perhaps his mum or dad was up and about trying to be quiet. The slow, repetitive shuffling outside his bedroom door sounded like someone cleaning the soles of their shoes on a doormat. Over and over and irritatingly over again, it drilled into Alfie's head, causing him to leap out of bed and fling open the bedroom door. There was no one there. The house was dark; the landing felt warm, but Alfie wasn't afraid. Closing the door, he returned to bed, pretending it was a weird dream and fell asleep.

The following evening, he was roused from sleep by the sound of footsteps. Definite, deliberate, heavy footsteps climbed the stairs to his bedroom door, stopped, descended to reascend and repeatedly descended and ascended. Each time the footsteps stopped outside his bedroom door, he held his breath, waited for a knock, and watched for a slow turning of the doorknob. But nothing happened.

At breakfast, Alfie mentioned hearing noises at night, but no one had heard anything. The footsteps he heard on the stairs were authentic, even if no one else heard them. Alfie knew that but kept it all to himself. He knew he wasn't dreaming.

Then, one night, the footsteps stopped outside Alfie's bedroom door on the first ascent. He held his breath. Three soft knocks pierced the silence. Someone wanted admittance.

Alfie, surprisingly unafraid, opened the door and felt a familiar shadow float in and fill the room with its numinous presence. Closing the bedroom door, Alfie turned in the quiet darkness to face his visitor. Slowly, an ethereal glow coloured his bedroom, from which a figure materialized to stand smiling at him. Bobby, who had disappeared five years ago without a trace, was in the room with him. His presence was striking, authentic and astonishing. Recognition passing in a flash was replaced with overwhelming feelings of remorse. He stood nakedly honest before his friend, his besmirched soul needing cleansing.

It was like an out-of-body experience for Alfie. A consuming weariness forced him to lie on the bed. Bobby approached and sat on the edge of Alfie's bed as friends sometimes do when visiting the sick. Alfie momentarily felt trapped. He couldn't speak, didn't know what to say, and didn't know what to do. Without imagination, he lay immobile, all his thoughts compressed into the here and now—this moment.

Breathing demanded all his attention. Vividly, he remembered the Saturday he saw Bobby beckoning to him from Milford and Rodgers across the street and his confusion and disappointment when Bobby disappeared.

Bobby was smiling at Alfie. It was not a vindictive smile but a smile full of warmth and affection. Then he spoke. Quietly and distinctly.

"Alfie, you have not been at peace with yourself since my disappearance. I have returned to bring you and my mother peace, interior peace of heart, soul and mind. Coming back is an arduous undertaking. I have put at risk my place in eternity, my afterlife, but I do it to see you and my mother one last time, to tell you that I love you and that we will be together again forever.

"On that Saturday five years ago, I hid in a chest full of strange stuff and was no sooner inside it when someone sealed it and somehow secreted it out of the store and transported it away. Taken by mistake, I disappeared. Later, when they opened the chest, my captors discovered me dead. I'd suffocated. They dumped me in a bog somewhere.

"It wasn't your fault, Alfie. There was nothing you or anyone could do. Stop blaming yourself. Please.

"What I have learned and want to tell you is that our eternal life begins from the moment of conception. Alfie, you are living your eternal life now. As am I. The only person you have to live with now is yourself. We will be together again.

"There is something I want you to do for me. My mother is more astute than you think. She is concerned about you and your future. Talk to her. Please."

Bobby's healing words cauterized Alfie's feelings of guilt, self-pity and deception. It was like a disinfectant 'grace' gently purging his soul. When Alfie raised his head and opened his eyes, Bobby was gone. The bedroom was in darkness. Alfie thought he had been dreaming for a moment but knew he hadn't. He felt liberated and unburdened, just as he had felt in the chapel when he lit a candle and prayed.

Alfie continued lighting the candles for Bobby's mother and noticed her health deteriorating. She was dying. It seemed to be taking a long time. Bobby's request, *Talk to her, talk to her,* hammered into his head. How could he face her and confess his sin of omission, his disingenuousness? He knew it was what he had to do to let her die in peace.

It was a Saturday afternoon. Sarah was in bed when Alfie called in to see her. He'd been to the chapel lighting the candles. Her dozy eyes brightened when she saw Alfie. He looked into his second mother's eyes and started to talk. A flood of words poured from his heart.

"I waited for him. I was the last one to leave. I searched for him everywhere I could think of, around the back and in the Smithy; I knew something wasn't right. It wasn't like him, I knew, I knew that. I gave up too soon; I didn't search long enough. I should have come here looking for him and told you everything. Then, we would have known he was still in the store and raised the alarm. I'm sorry."

A torrent of words like molten lava laden with remorse spewed out of Alfie's mouth. Bobby's mother listened as the river of lava calmed and slowed. She took Alfie's hand in hers and, caressing it gently, said, "Son, it won't have mattered if you had come here first; Bobby was already gone, he told me."

"You know, but…"

"All I want you to know before I go to Bobby is that I don't blame you for anything, and I don't want you to go on blaming yourself. Be at peace now. I am."

Her words, another cauterization, freeing him to live.

Sarah joined her son three months later to continue their eternal life together. Alfie became a missionary priest, spreading the good news far and wide. He is working in Africa today.

That is my story. I tell it every year on this day, wherever I can find a worthy audience.

The Tilley lamp went out, leaving the tin shed in total darkness. A flaming match appearing from nowhere relit the Tilley lamp. The little group huddled around it glanced nervously at each other.

"Who was that?" one asked.

"Do you think that was Bobby?" another proffered.

"I don't know," a few chorused.

"Let's search the place," another commanded.

The door of the tin hut was still secure. No one had left; if anyone had, they would have been seen. Anxiously, they searched, moving the bales of straw in the process. They found no one.

Milford and Rodgers store on Pound Street is long gone, as is the little tin shed in the field at the foot of the Mill Brae. But Bobby returns every year on All Souls Day to tell his story.

You must be in the right place and worthy at the right time.

After His Passing

After His Passing
they said
He was a lovely boy
humble and patient.
A steadfast friend
A great person to be with.

Funny, energetic and competent
talented and technically skilful
adaptable and willing
full of potential.

Caring for others
good with people
passionate concerning outdoors
a wonderful exemplar.

What I Thought at His Committal

Let me cry, Lord
Let me cry, Lord
Let me cry, Lord.
Let me scream
Yell away my tears
I tried
I tried,
I tried.
I didn't cry.
Now, I cry and cry silently.
Crosses
Crosses
Crosses.

Everyone, a prayer.

What's In a Name?

Jake Cordner reluctantly trailed behind his wife Maureen, snaking around the supermarket aisles, pushing a lightly laden trolley. It was mid-morning; shoppers, mainly seniors, shuffled around, passing their time. *Autumn is announcing its presence, and they're here, saving on the heating; why not?* Smiling, he thought of the library and other places where astute seniors and folk in fuel poverty might save on their heating bills.

He didn't want to be in a supermarket. Shopping was an occupation, it seemed to him, of browsing and, perchance, buying something. It wasn't his idea of time well spent. Jake's purchasing, generally born out of necessity, meant he knew what he wanted and where to get it at the best price. *What's the use of having a shopping list if you're going to debate with yourself on the choice of every item,* he thought, as his wife religiously hemmed and hawed along the aisles. The loud, overbearingly cheerful Christmas background music failed to lift Jake's spirits; quite the opposite, he wanted to get out of earshot as soon as possible.

Brain fogged, trailing behind Maureen on their third lap of the aisles, he noticed a woman with a child, scooping nuts into a bag. Edging closer for a better look, they were, he thought, *hazelnuts.* Curiosity satisfied, returning to duty, he trolleyed along behind his wife.

That evening, when conversation lulled, he mentioned the lady scooping up the hazelnuts in the supermarket.

"When I was a boy, Maureen, I used to go foraging for hazelnuts at this time of year."

"Really ?"

"The walk alongside the Inver River where the narrow gauge railway used to be; we walked along the railway line for miles gathering hazel nuts from the bushes hedging it. When we were a little older, we walked to Craiginorne nut braes to gather nuts. It was a good walk, about five miles."

"What did you do with the nuts?"

"We ate most of them on the way home. I'm lucky to have a tooth left in my mouth, cracking them open. The leftovers mum used in cakes and things. I fancy a trip up there, for old times' sake. Want to come? It's only a five-minute drive."

The afternoon sky was moody when they set off on the dual carriageway to Craiginorne. Jake's eyes searched for the familiar left turn that would take them to the nut braes but didn't find it, muttering to himself as he drove, "I should have taken a left there; how did I miss it?"

Jake had bicycled up the Ballymena Road to Craiginorne on his last nut-foraging outing. But that was a long time ago. This time, he was driving on a new dual carriageway that, in its construction, required the restructuring of miner road intersections, much to the confusion of the unfamiliar, like Jake.

Ahead, seeing the signed turn-off for Ballyboley, he took it, aware that Ballyboley was on the opposite side of the dual carriageway from where he wanted to go. Exiting left, he had another choice: follow the sign, cross the flyover to Ballyboley or proceed straight ahead and explore. *At least, straight ahead,* he thought, *we'll be on the same side as Craiginorne.*

Another decision. Right or left? It was a no-brainer; left would take him back towards Craiginorne. Ignoring the invitation to visit Ballyboley, it was a short distance up the stem of a t-junction to join the Ballygowan Road. They motored slowly, like tourists, along the narrow country road, wondering what was around the next bend. It was a new, unexplored wonderland on their doorstep.

New as it was to Jake, a sense of déjà vu, faint at first, increased as he drove along. His mind searched for associations and connections. Suddenly, the road came to a dead end. They could go no further. Parked up, they sat silently overlooking the dual carriageway below as the traffic whizzed past. The nut braes weren't far away on their right, but they would have to walk over rough terrain to get there. Stymied, Jake turned and drove back the way they had come.

A glimpse of a roadside sign on his left compelled him to stop and reverse. Leaning across Maureen, Jake read the sign aloud:

Clements Wood

National Trust

Welcome.

"I had a sense of place when we turned onto this road. I could feel it. I felt drawn to it. It's weird, Maureen."

"What is Jake?"

"The name Maureen! The name."

"What? I don't get it."

"It's a long story. You've heard it. No? You must have forgotten, then. When I was a child, I often heard it said that our family name should be Clements. I thought it was a joke and never gave it a second thought. Now, fate finds us here at Clements Wood. It's creepy, don't you think?"

"I think it's a load of old tosh, Jake. Your imagination has taken flight again, but since we've come this far, we might as well explore the woods. Who knows what we'll find? We might be in for a big surprise." Laughing, she took his arm.

Another sign informed them that The Woodland Trust had acquired the land from a local farmer, hence the name Clements and that in former times, it was a popular stopping-off point for mystery bus tours from Larne into the countryside.

Leaving Clements Wood, Maureen drew Jake's attention to the unassuming little church nestling in a hollow below the road.

Looking down on it, Jake was bemused. "This is the weirdest experience I've ever had, Maureen."

"What?"

"I'll explain later; let's see if we can go in. Shall we?"

In size and atmosphere, it was more a chapel than a church. Jake sensed a wholesome prayerfulness drawing him in. Maureen ambled around, surveying the interior. Jake sat in a pew at the rear of the knave, letting the childhood banter about his family surname filter through his mind in search of substance. He hadn't summoned the images. They just happened. He couldn't control them. When the spool of thoughts abruptly ceased, Jake thought, *is there any substance to it? Why was I drawn to this place? What am I supposed to do? Is there unfinished business here making demands on me?* It was as if he was appealing to a higher authority for guidance.

Maureen, her tour around the chapel completed, sat beside Jake, remarking, "It's hushed here, almost monastic. It's like a kind of time capsule."

"Yes, quiet and empty, but full of welcome. It's a holy place; can't you feel it? It speaks to you. I feel bound to this place as a prisoner to his chains. I can't explain it. The hairs on my neck stood up when I walked through the door. It's scary."

Setting his feelings aside, Jake viewed the stained glass memorial windows dotted around the church, eloquently articulating the devotion of folk who had worshipped there. Some had obvious connections with Larne, but one with the surname Gorteen interested Jake because he had seen the name before on one of his walks around the town. A coincidence? Try as he might, he couldn't place where he had come across it and moved on. Jake's attention zeroed in on the sanctuary and altar. Something about them searched his deep well of memory but made no connection.

Outside, they toured the neat little burial ground, reading the headstones and mentally noting dates. The earliest gravestone they could read was 1817. It was silent; nothing moved as they walked through a history they knew nothing about.

Jake was scribbling a note on a piece of paper when he heard Maureen's voice excitingly beckoning.

"Look at this, Jake," she said, pointing to the inscription on a headstone.

"What?"

"The name, Jake! It's my surname, Cordner nee Shields."

The inscription read, *John Shields, Castlewellan 1878.*

"Is that a coincidence, too, Jake? Or are we both drawn here to serve some purpose?"

"I don't know, Maureen, but it feels like it. I sense this burial ground's ancestry."

"Could there possibly be any connection?"

"Hard to know; you'll have to check your family history."

"It seems we're both on a journey of discovery, Jake."

Jake's eyes followed the path leading upwards to the narrow country road and beyond to the wooded hills that seamlessly blended into the blue sky above. After listening to an uplifting sermon, he wondered if the congregation, after Mass, floated up the path on a tsunami of religious fervour to the heavens above. An image of Elijah in a flaming chariot on his way to paradise flashed across his mind. Elisha's statement, *where you go, I go,* screamed out to him. Jake closed his eyes to erase the images, telling himself, *this is weird.* I came here on a nostalgic impulse to gather nuts, and now I feel I'm going nuts. It's surreal. First, the name Clements pops up, and then the church. It's as if I'm being led; *where I have been, you will follow.*

On the narrow road, looking back down the path, he could feel the faithful hurrying past in nervous anticipation on their way into Mass.

He was shaking his head and smiling when Maureen joined him. "Could it possibly be true, Maureen?"

"What?"

"The story I heard told so often as a child about my grandfather."

"I don't know; you'll have to tell me again."

"I will, but first, I've got something to explore. Okay?"

"Okay," Maureen agreed, intrigued. The couple walked back to the car.

***

Christmas had come and gone, followed by the New Year heralding new beginnings. Sitting by the fire reading her book, Maureen was interrupted by Jake emerging from the cubby hole he called his study.

"Job done, I think, Maureen. You won't believe what I'm going to tell you," he announced reflectively.

"What are you going to tell me?"

"The family story. It all fits. Well, the pertinent bits do. It has to be true."

"Enlighten me."

"Okay, but first, there are a couple of things that are pivotal to the authenticity of this story. I have spent weeks, as you know, trawling through the family history. I unearthed my grandfather's birth, marriage and baptism certificates, and more. In the roof space of my mother's house, behind the water cistern, I found a bag containing lots of papers and my grandfather's notebook. It's a precious find."

"What possessed you to search your mother's roof space?"

"My mother suggested it. She said dad was forever putting stuff up there out of the way."

"Well?"

"My grandfather's surname was Clements."

"Really?"

"Yes, that's what it says on his birth certificate, but that's not all. There is a suggestion that he may have only been a half-brother to his siblings. That's where it gets murky. But he was also a master mason. Okay?"

"Are you sure?"

"As sure as I can be. It's on his birth certificate. I checked the dates. They fit, and he wrote about his work as a mason."

"That's it then. Job done?"

"Not quite. There's more; I'm not called Clements."

"No. Right. Why not?"

"Good question. My grandfather changed his name to Cordner. That's why I'm a Cordner, not a Clements. What do you make of that?"

"I've no idea what to think. It's too much to take in. Are you sure?"

"Yes, I'm sure. I have all the paperwork. It's on William's baptism certificate and marriage certificate. He was baptised and married on the same date in a Catholic church. He changed his religion as well as his name. It's incredible but true."

"One thing didn't fit. The sanctuary and altar in the Ballygowan church are not marble; they're hardwood. In the family story, they're marble. But that's sorted too, and it all fits together."

"How did you discover that?"

"Well, when a lot of online searching got me precisely nowhere, I got the courage to ask the parish priest for help. He kindly obliged, and after searching the parish records and talking to some of his parishioners, he confirmed that the Ballygowan Church had a marble sanctuary and altar. What about that? It confirms what my grandfather wrote in his notebook and more."

"Okay. Now, are you going to tell me the story?"

"I'll try. You're not going to believe it. It took me a while to get my head around it.

"By the end of the 17th century, agents of the State rigorously enforced the Penal Laws in Ireland; the closure of the monasteries denied Catholics places to worship. Father Edmund Moore, in 1770, assumed clerical responsibility for a vast swathe of County Antrim stretching along the coast from Belfast, far beyond Glenarm. Pastoral care was secretly administered. In a secluded glen in Ballygowan near Larne, there was a mass rock that Father Moore used to celebrate Mass.

"In 1787, the current Larne, Carrickfergus and Ballyclare parishes formed one huge parish covering much of East Antrim. With the mantle of Penal Laws receding, the parish priest, now a Father McCary, built the first post-reformation churches in the new parish, the church in Ballygown and a temporary church in Carrickfergus.

"This background note is important, Maureen, because it puts Ballygowan at the centre of Catholic worship in the region. There was a church, a school, and a consecrated burial ground. It was an autonomous, growing Catholic community. Two decades elapsed before a make-shift Catholic church was built on

Mucket Hill in Larne in 1807. In 1852, Ballygowan and Larne formed a new parish. Maureen that explains the longstanding association between Ballygowan and Larne.

"Then, in 1869, Ballyclare and Ballygowan formed a new parish. To accommodate the increasing number of souls, The Holy Family Church in Ballygowan was refurbished and modernised in 1932. The work included the installation of a new marble sanctuary and an altar. The installation cost for the sanctuary and altar was five-hundred pounds. Maureen, in 1932, that was a lot of money. With inflation, today's price could be between ten and twenty *thousand* pounds.

"My grandfather, William Clements, a master mason, was employed to install the sanctuary and altar. He dithered at first, being a Unitarian, on taking on the task, but his desire to work with marble prevailed. He was a single, fit and healthy young man and bicycled daily to Ballygown. The Italian architect overseeing the sanctuary and altar installation spoke little English. William spoke Ulster Scots. Fortunately, the parish priest at the time, having studied at the Irish College in Rome, could facilitate conversation between the architect and the master mason, who estimated that the installations would take him a week to complete.

"On a Monday morning in 1932, William presented at the Holy Family Church in Ballygowan, bright and early, keen to make a start. The sound of silence greeted him. Parking his bicycle and tools by the entrance, he tried the door and, finding it open, entered the church. It was his first time in a Catholic church. It felt different to his church, less austere, more compassionate, or simply different. With practically all of the refurbishment and modernisation work completed, all that remained was the installation of the sanctuary and altar.

"'You're here before us, I see, William,' the parish priest greeted him before introducing his dapper companion, the Italian architect. Much of the morning was spent by William poring over the detailed architectural drawings spread on the floor with the architect, seeking clarification as needed. The conference concluded, William was left to begin the sanctuary installation on the understanding that the architect and parish priest would meet with him again on Tuesday morning.

"Alone in the church, William worked diligently until his grumbling tummy suggested sustenance. It was well past lunchtime; the time had slipped by unnoticed. Munching on his sandwich, he wandered around, familiarising himself with the modest little church, and when pangs of hunger were satisfied, William returned to work.

"The afternoon passed quietly outside, the light inside slowly faded, and a monastic ambience filled the church. If William had felt it, simplicity would have adequately described it, a comfortable feeling of clarity. The dimming light made the precision fitting of the marble pieces in place more demanding. Pausing to take stock, he sensed the subtle ambient changes, but he needed better light to fit one more marble piece into its place before calling it a day. Fortunately, two large candles were at hand beside the sanctuary. William fixed the marble piece neatly into place by the light of the candles placed on either side of where it was to go.

"Satisfied, he settled in a pew to consider his work plan for Tuesday. Then, standing in the church's nave, he cast a master mason's keen eye over his day's work. The burning candles captured his eyes. The yellow guttering flames danced in a sea of luminosity, raising his gaze heavenwards towards the source of eternal light. He blinked several times and rubbed his eyes but couldn't erase the illusions. The buoyancy of the rising flickering flames bore him higher and higher until he floated on his back in a current of imagination on a warm, tranquil sea. Closing his eyes, he fastened on the moment. When he opened his eyes, the church was in total darkness; only a faint smell of burnt candle wax lingered.

"Convinced he had nodded off for a few minutes, and assuming the candles had self-extinguished, William packed up his tools and left the church. Outside, a brooding evening sky shrouded his niggling apprehension all the way home.

"That night, in a dream, he saw a ball of flame and heard a voice calling out from the middle of it;

'William! William, come to me.'

'I can't, I can't; it's too hot. It's too hot,' William heard himself respond.

"Provoked from sleep, wondering how long the angst of his dream would last, a slow suffusion of peace returned him to restful slumber.

"On Tuesday morning, the architect and the parish priest, content with William's progress, quickly dealt with any queries and left him to get on with the job. In the afternoon, the monastic ambience again filled the church. It seemed to filter in through the stone floor and walls. William didn't notice for a while until he thought he heard voices. Thinking it was the architect and parish priest returning, he glanced around, but the church was empty and eerily quiet. William thought it was probably folk visiting the burial ground outside and settled back to work.

"Not long settled, he heard the voices again. William downed tools and listened to the voices. They were pleading voices coming, it seemed, from different places in the church. Then, the voices faded away, leaving the church silent. Intrigued, William walked around the knave, searching for an explanation. Was it an echo? Was it birds on the roof?

"Passing a stained glass window, hearing a whisper, William paused, turned to face the window and read the inscription. *'Pray for the deceased relatives of…'* as he read the words, he heard the emotional pleading of the petitioner, no longer a whisper, loud and clear in his mind. Momentarily transfixed, uncertain he could trust his senses, William stood confounded until reason cleared his mind. At the adjacent stained glass window, he experienced the same sensation. The petition began *'pray for the souls of…'* Noticing the dates, he realised that the petitioner was now appealing for prayers from the grave. *Is that possible? Can we pray for the dead? Can they reciprocate?* He asked himself.

"Bemused and slightly unsettled, William's tour of the rest of the memorial stained glass windows yielded similar moving experiences. Unfamiliar with this form of communing with and on behalf of the dead, he nonetheless found it reassuring, a well of hope. Halfway through his tour, he heard voices all around chanting, *'Save us, saviour of the world,'* over and over again. It sounded to William as if those buried around the church, joining in, were forming a colossal petitionary wave. At that moment, he became acutely aware of the mystery of salvation, of being one with everyone who had ever lived and would ever live. At the last window, the pleading quietened until the voices drifting away became inaudible, and silence filled the church.

"William's sleep was peaceful that night. Then, as images of creation invaded his mind, it became restless and finally turbulent as he wrestled with an unknown assailant.

'What is your name?' his assailant asked.

'William,' he answered.

'Change your name.'

'I don't want to.'

'Do as I command.'

"He wrestled valiantly with his assailant throughout the night, but morning could not be postponed. Bicycling to Bally-gown, his search for meaning in his dream was fruitless. A feeling settled on him that it was some omen and that nothing would be the same again, nothing, logic or sense. A thought fleeted across his mind to mention his experiences in the church and his dreams to the parish priest, but it drifted off into an empty sea.

"Progress on the installation of the sanctuary had gone well. On Wednesday morning, William informed the architect and the parish priest that he expected to finish it that evening. It was approaching lunchtime when he completed the sanctuary struc-ture, leaving only the Tabernacle and the ornate marble capping piece to be set in place to finish the installation.

"After lunch, he removed the Tabernacle from its protective covering and gingerly slotted it into place; it was a seamless fit. Pleased, he set about fixing the five capping pieces in place. The centre capping piece over the Tabernacle was more ornate than the others and was the last piece of the sanctuary William put in place.

"Absorbed in putting the tabernacle capping piece in place, Jake didn't notice or feel the atmosphere in the church subtly changing. The church's interior dimmed as the afternoon shad-ows crept around the burial ground.

"Standing back, astonished, in the diming nave, he couldn't believe what he saw. Feeling dizzy, looking at the sanctuary, lit like a stage set, his legs weakening, he sat in a pew. Subtle rain-bow hues highlighting and harmonising the marble's natural colours, moved in a sublime choreography around the sanctu-ary. But there was more, much more. Figures danced up and down on either side of the Tabernacle in celebration. He could hear music. *Are they angels?* He thought. *What else could they be?* He sat for a long time in the surrounding darkness, watching the angels happily dancing around the Tabernacle, resisting the urge to join in but strangely at peace with himself.

"The sound of the church door opening and closing stirred William. The dancing angels disappeared. The parish priest and the architect were returning eagerly to see the finished sanctuary. They were pleased with what they saw. William didn't mention what he'd seen.

"That night, he had another dream, a dream with a twist that was so real. He was doing his job, building a sanctuary in a cathedral. As the marble crept up the backing structure, scaffolding was needed, a lot of scaffolding, for William to construct the sanctuary to the specified height, tens of yards above the cathedral floor. In his dream, he was continuously ladder climbing to reach the level of the scaffolded platform. He had never climbed as high before. There seemed no end to it. Then, climbing higher, he entered a fleecy white cloud, emerging into a sublime soft white inviting light. Perfect light. Jake was in a behavioural loop in the dream, continuously climbing ladders to reach the perfect light.

"On Thursday morning, William rose, carefree, eager to get up to Ballygowan to start work on the altar. The altar was a simple enough structure. The marble altar top rested on two plinths. He marked out the positions for the plinths on the floor and waited for the architect and parish priest to arrive and approve the layout, which they did after they had inspected the sanctuary in better light.

"With the plinths built, William had to wait for them to harden before fixing the marble facings on Friday. He had gathered his tools, preparing to call it a day when the parish priest came in to see how he was getting on. Chatting with William, the parish priest sketched the history of the Holy Family Church and what it meant to the local community. William, in his dissonant way, confessed that it was a place that spoke to him.

'You're not the only one who felt the pull of this place, William; lots of folks felt it,' the parish priest informed him.

"William, curious, probed, asking if anyone had told him how the church spoke to them. The answer he got was *all sorts of ways*, and sensing there was much the parish priest wasn't saying, William let the matter drop.

"The next morning, with his sleep, uninterrupted, William rose earlier than usual, eager to return to Ballygown and finish the altar. He was experiencing the pull of the place without realising it.

"Fitting and fixing the marble panels to the plinths demanded attention to detail and meticulous precision. After lunch, with the aid of two brawny parishioners' willing hands, William oversaw the placement of the marble altar top on the plinths in the presence of the parish priest and architect. It was, in every respect, a ceremonial occasion.

"William bicycled away from Ballygown content, satisfied that he had done something that needed to be done with his mind firmly set on a return visit. He didn't go out as usual on Friday night to meet his friends. He stayed in. Ballygowan church was tugging at him. It seemed reluctant to let him go.

"That night, he dreamt he stood alone, speechless, before his God. His every fault, failure and misdemeanour in his life, barefacedly, brazenly, paraded before him, compelling him to plead for mercy, begging to renew his joy, cleanse his heart, and wash his soul. In the background, the Ballygowan church's memorial windows, one by one, with the chorus of voices from the surrounding burial ground, lent support to his petition.

"In the following weeks and months, William was busy as usual. There was no noticeable change in his demeanour; only those close with the capability to discern minute behavioural transiences could have noticed. He was pondering the reality of God.

"Six months after completing the Ballygown church sanctuary and altar installations, William left home to work in the north of England. He was 28. William, drawn to churches, worked on many historic buildings, including Durham Cathedral and St. Nicholas Cathedral in Newcastle upon Tyne.

"At work, he met an old monk, a Cistercian, Father Phillip, who he describes as a good, wise scholar, someone he could trust in his search for enlightenment on the reality of God. Many conversations followed. William acquainted the old monk with his experiences in the church in Ballygowan, including the sequence of dreams. Each of his situational experiences and related dreams he discovered had biblical connotations. Father Phillip, a good listener, perceiving that William's rather impersonal relationship with God had become very real and deeply personal, could sense an easing of tension, a coming together, a unity in him.

"William met Ethel Cordner, a catholic girl. They fell in love, married and set up a home in Newcastle upon Tyne. He was 30 years old; Ethel was 28. The intriguing thing is that William changed both his names. He substituted his fiancé's surname, Cordner, for Clements and Jacob for his Christian name, William. That's where the name Jacob Cordner enters the family lineage. I have the marriage and baptism certificates to prove it. There's more. The marriage and baptism certificates are dated the same. Jacob was accepted into the Catholic church the day he married his beloved Ethel.

"There is nothing in his notes to explain the name changes. I suspect he may have been searching for his other parent. It would have been difficult back then to search the records, and even if he could, he would only have ended up as I did, with an incomplete birth certificate. However, there is also the possibility that someone who knew the truth told him.

"Perhaps he didn't want to burden anybody with explanations. I can only surmise that his time in the Ballygowan church refreshed his need to know, and he became a pilgrim without realising it. Remember the dreams he had. He was searching for something and felt the pull of the church towards God. Could it have been the dream in which he was commanded to change his name? I don't know.

"My grandfather and grandmother had three children: a boy and two girls. My father, the firstborn, was named Jacob. Then, the war wrecked everyone's lives.

"After the war, my father, family in tow, returned to his roots as Jacob Cordner. I am Jacob the Third. There were folk alive then, with second-hand knowledge of my grandfather's history, hence the banter in our home about the family name. It was all a long time ago.

"It's inconceivable. Isn't it? How a woman bagging hazelnuts in a supermarket could have opened me to the fullness of this experience. I know who I am and have a fuller sense of place. Bombs demolished the marble sanctuary and altar my grandfather built in Ballygowan church. Fortunately, some things are indestructible. I feel the pull of the place, a part of it, a place of silence in a hidden glen.

"It is sad that I never really knew my grandfather. I only saw him once or twice. I know him better now; he was a man of faith. What's in a name in the meaninglessness of time?"

Mary's Story

A teacher asked her class to explain in writing how they got
their chosen name.

Mary 7 ½, in her jotter, wrote:

My mummy called me

Mary after God's mother.

She called me Helena

After Saint Helena who

found the true cross.

God's mother is the

Greatest woman in the world.

Her mother treasured Mary's jotter page.

A Night to Remember

It was a typical February day, short, dull, cold and grey; bitterly cold and grey. There was no sun, not even a hint. It didn't bother Willie McFaul; he was hard at work weatherproofing a roof before calling it a day. The light was fading fast. Soon, it would be too dark to work. He frequently paused to blow warm breath into cupped, numbed hands, before continuing, slate by slate. The low, feeble sun was long set when, by the light of the moon in a threatening sky, he slowly, rung by rung, climbed down the ladder to the ground. Leaning, his back against the ladder, Willie began gingerly peeling his stiffened fingers, one by one, off the shaft of his hammer, doggedly grasped in his left hand. Bits of hardened skin marked the spread of his fingers on the wooded shaft. A self-employed builder, Willie was repairing a fire-damaged house in the hinterland of Ballyboley.

When the snow started falling, he flexed his fingers and rubbed his hands together forcefully to encourage blood flow and feeling. Big, soft snowflakes billowed from the gathering ceiling of low, menacing clouds. It was quiet, not a sound, as flakes of snow filled the sky, drifting down, mantling everything in white. Stillness settled around the farmhouse as if in expectation. The slated roof quickly became like a white blanket covering the house, and the snow-laden branches of the trees silhouetted around the farmyard hung heavy. Movement among the trees caught his attention. He stared hard but saw nothing.

It was six o'clock when he turned the key in the ignition after clearing the snow off the windscreen of his old VW Passat hatchback that doubled as a work van. The starter gurgled and groaned. He tried again. There was more gurgling and groaning, but this time, it sounded terminal. Exasperated, he banged the dashboard with his fist before collecting himself, earnestly apologising to the Passat. They'd been together a long time; it owed him nothing, and he didn't want to lose it. Calmed, composed, silent prayer offered to the Passat Gods, Willie tried again. His old friend cleared its throat and reluctantly came to life.

Unaccustomed to navigating the narrow country roads during the day, Willie was anxious about driving on unfamiliar, unlit, narrow byways in a snowstorm. Slowly, he negotiated the way down the tractor-rutted lane that wound its way down to the main road. Willie gripped the steering wheel as firmly as he'd grasped his hammer on the roof, and greatly relieved, he joined the Ballymena Road, leaving Ballboley in his wake.

He thought, *we're on our way home now*, still cautiously driving through the deepening snow as the Passat searched for grip. Traffic would pack the dry snow hard, forming an icy crust making driving conditions more hazardous. But Willie was content that his old Passat was up to the job, and they would soon be home safe and sound in Ballygally.

The engine started sputtering. Willie glanced at the petrol gauge on the dashboard; it registered half full. *It could be dirty petrol, dampness, or anything,* he thought. No, it couldn't, he told himself; it would have shown up sooner. As suddenly as the engine's sputtering started, the sputtering stopped. Willie mouthed a silent prayer.

A gritter rushed past, spewing out its mixture of salt and grit. The sight and sounds were reassuring, even though Willie knew it would take time for the salt and grit to affect hard-packed snow. He was approaching Millbrook when the headlights started flickering, and the warning lights on the dashboard began blinking. "What the hell is going on?" He asked himself. "What am I going to do?" Willie was beginning to think he might not make it home, and to compound his woe, he'd left his mobile phone at home. *Must be a loose connection*, he thought. Then the dashboard settled, and the headlights stopped flickering.

Millbrook junction was not far up the road. Willie usually took a left for the inland route to Ballygally, but not tonight, he decided. It was a no-brainer. He thought, *it's better to stick to the main roads; they'll be gritted. Drive through the town onto the Coast Road home.*

He had driven past Chaine Park when the engine started sputtering again like it was suffering a severe bronchial infection. The Passat shook and shivered towards the Black Arch. It sounded terminal. *But we're getting there, not too far to go now; I can walk it if I have to,* Willie thought. He stopped to let a gritter bustle through the Arch. The rest did the Passat good; it miraculously cleared its tubes. Turning left at the Castle and left again, he was within sight of home if he could have seen it through the falling snow. But Willie knew where he was. With the Passat safely garaged, he silenced the engine and sighed, letting his anxiety dissipate. He was thankful to be safely home, and sure he would not be venturing out again.

Willie was hardly through the door when Mary rushed to meet him, and unburdened herself.

"Willie, what kept you? You're usually home earlier than this. What a day I've had."

"There's a blizzard out there, Mary," Willie muttered, shedding his fur-lined beanie and donkey jacket.

Sat on the bottom of the stairs, he unlaced his work boots, eased them off and started vigorously rubbing his ice-cold feet before donning the waiting slippers, listening as Mary filled him in on all her day's activities. It was a daily ritual, exchanging their days' happenings, but it usually occurred across the dinner table.

Raising his head, he looked up at Mary. Her long red hair, splayed around her shoulders, backlit by the hall ceiling light, shimmered, forming a very light red ring around the back of her head, gradually changing the hue around her face into a dark reddish mantle. *Your grandmother was right*, he thought, *when she told you never to hide your beautiful red hair.* He wondered if that advice was the catalyst that made Mary the outgoing, non-judgemental person she is: herself. Mary had a way with people. She could tune in, hold fast to the connection, listen, make acquaintances feel worth something, be uplifted, and all the better for their time together.

Willie, in many ways, envied Mary. He wasn't anti-social; he just wasn't good at small talk. It was part of Mary's DNA to embrace the well-being of her neighbours. *One for each day of the year*, he often thought. Willie liked things planned. He would hesitate to do the unplanned, the unexpected. A prisoner of routine, it could be said. If there were a problem, he would address it head-on, seeking a solution. Willie got things done. Empathy was something Mary was teaching Willie. But if someone in need approached Willie for help, he wouldn't hesitate to render whatever assistance he could. In emergencies, he would react spontaneously.

"Wait till I tell you," Mary continued. "I went to visit Marjorie, auch God help her, she hadn't seen anyone in a couple of days. So I took her and her wee dog for a bit of a walk up to the park. She was okay; she managed that, and I'm glad I did before the snow came. It might be a day or two before she gets out again. The house beside hers is up for sale, you know? I hope she gets good neighbours; she deserves them. She was asking about you, by the way."

As Mary's monologue continued, Willie sat like a rabbit caught in a car's headlights.

"I did a wee bit of shopping for her. Her fridge was nearly empty. It's a pity living there alone with all her family gone. I wouldn't like that, you know."

Willie did know. Mary had told him often enough. They were fortunate their family was all around them. He and Mary had nothing to concern themselves about. Mary would be well looked after if and when that time came. He had seen to it.

Mary, interrupting Willie's wandering thoughts, carried on chronicling her day, "Then I went over to see Isobel. She's not very well, you know Willie. I'm worried about her living alone."

"Why? Isn't she living in a sheltered housing facility with wardens?"

"Yes, but I'm not sure it's 24/7 cover if you know what I mean. At times, Isobel seems dizzy and confused. She hasn't any family I can talk to."

"Someone must have decided that she was capable of living on her own; otherwise, she wouldn't be there."

"But, but…"

"No buts, Mary. If you are worried about Isobel, go over to-morrow, weather permitting, and see how she is, and if you still feel as you do now, have a quiet word with the warden. Some-body has to be keeping an eye on her."

"I know, but I am concerned about her, Willie."

"Mary, there's nothing we can do about it tonight. Let's sleep on it and talk it over tomorrow. I've had a rough old day, love, and I'm knackered, okay?"

Over supper, Willie told Mary his relief at getting the building he was working on weatherproof before the snow came. He shared his concerns regarding his faithful old Passat now sheltering comfortably in the garage, wondering if it would be fit for purpose in the morning, weather permitting. If it was, would the roads to Ballyboley be passable? Reluctantly, he confessed to Mary that perhaps it was time to say goodbye to the Passat. Outside, the snow stealthily deepened.

Settled in front of their wood-burning stove, Mary and Willie chatted. They didn't notice the time passing until Mary said, "I'll get ready for bed while you do whatever you must, okay?"

It was just past midnight. Willie went into his little office, checked his answer service for any messages and emails and dealt with other bits and pieces that needed his attention before heading to the bathroom and bed.

Mary was reading when Willie snuggled in beside her. She felt warm and comfortable. A weird thought flashed across Willie's mind. Something his mother told him years ago about her conversation with a widowed neighbour. His mother, not long married, had been feeling homesick. To lift her spirits, her widowed neighbour had said, "Sure you'll be alright, love. If you were like me, it'd be a warm body you'd be looking for."

Willie never fully appreciated the depth of meaning in that remark and laughed at the thought.

"What's so funny, Willie?"

"Just a thought, love. Just a silly thought."

When Mary switched her bedside light off, it was far past midnight. Outside, the snow was still silently falling.

The sound of bells ringing forced Willie awake. *It's the intruder alarms*, he thought; *Mary's gone downstairs and forgot to deactivate the intruder alarm.* Sitting upright in the bed, blinking furiously to drive the sleep from his eyes, he saw Mary sitting beside him, telephone in hand, listening.

"Your lights are off? All of them?" Mary asks.

(Mary listens)

"Are you sure?" Mary mouths to Willie, "It's Isobel; her lights have gone off."

(Mary cuts Isobel off)

"Did you try the other rooms?"

(Mary listens)

"Have you looked outside?"

(Mary waits, shrugging her shoulders, and looks at Willie.)

"Ok, the street lights are out. Can you see to move around?"

(Mary butts in)

"Where are you now?"

(Mary listens)

"In the kitchen?"

(Mary, listening, looks at Willie.)

"What are you doing in the kitchen?"

(Mary listens)

"You went into the kitchen to make yourself a cup of tea."

(Mary butts in)

"Is that when the lights went out?"

(Mary listens)

"Did you make tea?"

(Mary listens)

"Where are you now?"

(Mary apologetically interjects)

"Sorry, I know you're beside the phone. Are you in your bed-room?"

(Mary, listening, raises her eyebrows at Willie)

"Isobel, I want you to return to the kitchen and turn every-thing off. Everything, do you understand everything? Okay?"

(Mary anxiously waits)

"Right, you've done that. There's probably a fault some-where. Get back into bed; you're safer there, and try to get some sleep. Everything will be back to normal in the morning. I'll ring you in the morning to check, okay?"

(Mary waits)

"You're in bed, Isobel. Good. Good night. I'll ring you in the morning."

Mary put the phone down, and Willie relieved it wasn't the intruder alarm, waited to be brought up to speed on Isobel's lack of lighting. He didn't have long to wait.

"That was Isobel. She got up to make herself a cup of tea, and her lights went out. So she rang me to see if our lights were out, too. As far as I can tell, all the lights in her building and the street lights are out. I got her to ensure that everything in the kitchen was switched off and told her to get into bed and try to sleep. What do you think?"

"How's she making her way around her flat?"

"She keeps a torch by her bed for emergencies."

"Why did she ring you?"

"She has my number."

"I know she has your number, Mary; otherwise, she couldn't have rung you," he irritably responded. "Why did she ring you? Did she ring the warden?"

"I don't know if she rang the warden. All I know is she rang me. Any port in a storm, I suppose. We're friends. Do you think she'll be all right?"

"Do we have a torch handy in case our lights go out?"

"No."

"Something to think about then. There could be lots of lights out tonight. But that was good advice you gave Isobel. She'll be all right; come on, let's try and get some sleep, love."

Willie slumped back into his pillow, reached for the duvet, pulled it up around them and, cosying up to Mary, tried to sleep. But he knew it was a lost cause. Mary wouldn't let herself sleep. He lay beside her, listening to her rapid breathing, feeling her body pulsing and quickening. Long, silent, sleepless minutes occupied the space between them until Mary's suppressed anxieties poured out.

"I'm worried about her alone in the dark, Willie."

"What? Why? Isobel's up there every night in the dark; what's special about tonight?"

"Her lights are out. If she awakens any other night, she can put the light on, right?"

"We sleep in the dark, don't we? Most people do. Look, there's a power line down somewhere or a transformer out of action; it'll be put right soon. There's nothing to worry about."

"I think I should go up to her just to be sure she's okay."

"Are you having a crisis of conscience? You have done everything you possibly could. Isobel is not your responsibility. Did she ring the warden? We don't know, do we? If she needed help, real emergency help, she must have numbers to ring, an alarm system of some sort."

"I know, Willie, I know, but I just can't lie here and do nothing."

"Mary, you have done everything you could. You have given

her sound advice. Think about it. What would you do up there? Do you have a key to let yourself in? Do you want Isobel to come downstairs by torchlight to let you in? Look outside; there's at least three inches of snow on the ground. You did the right thing. She's safer in bed."

Mary switched her bedside lamp off and lay beside Willie, but sleep wouldn't come.

"Willie, I can't sleep. I have to go up and see if Isobel is okay. Take the car out for me, please. I'll go; you needn't come."

"Mary, I told you about the car. I was lucky to get home. I don't know if it'll start?"

"Well, we could at least try. Couldn't we?"

"To do what if we get there? Throw pebbles at her window? It's not a Romeo and Juliet thing. Isobel's on the second floor. I thought it was sheltered housing. There must be somebody in charge?"

"Yes, she has the number. Maybe there's no one there. I don't know if it's 24/7 care. She's up there all on her own, Willie. God love her; she gets confused sometimes, and I'm afraid. Willie."

"Ok, ok, ok," Willie said, yielding against his better judgement.

He knew from experience that once Mary got something into her head, nothing would deter her. She had to see it through, even if it meant she might regret it afterwards. Some might say she was obstinate or thran, but Willie thought it was a character flaw with deep-seated roots; he chose to leave well enough alone.

Grumpily, he said, "We'll give it a go then and see what happens."

Suitably attired in warm clothing and feet booted, Willie made his way out to the garage to confront the Passat, thinking, *You won't be up for a run-out tonight in this weather, old friend. Will you?*

He was spot on in his assessment. The Passat wasn't up for it. When he turned the key in the ignition, the starter groaned as if woken from a deep sleep, but eventually the engine came to life. Relieved, Willie left the engine ticking over, the garage doors opened and went to fetch Mary.

Driving carefully through the deepening snow, acutely aware that their street would not be gritted, Willie let the Passat feel its way. He was watchful on the gritted Coast Road back to town, following in the fresh tracks of another vehicle.

Through the Black Arch, Willie thought he saw something on the road.

"What's that, Mary?" He asked, pointing ahead with his right hand. Mary couldn't see anything through the falling snow.

Willie flicked the headlights onto full beam, instantly filling the windscreen with blinding snow, forcing him immediately back onto dip. Peering fixedly ahead, leaning closer to the windscreen, Willie saw a shape forming in front of him through the falling snow. He was almost on it when he realised it was a car broadside on the road dead ahead. They had happened upon an accident. A car travelling towards the Black Arch had slewed across the road, mounting the footpath, coming to rest with its bonnet nestling against the iron railing, preventing it from tumbling into the sea. The snow tracks were fresh. The car lights were on.

"It's just happened, Mary, a few minutes ago! Oh my God!" Willie shouted.

He stopped beside the stricken car, leaving the Passat's lights on, turned on his hazard lights and leapt out. "Mary, there's someone in the car," Willie yelled.

Opening the stricken car's door, he found a man slumped over the steering wheel with the deflated airbag all over him. He wasn't moving or making a sound. Willie was sure he was dead.

"Ring 999, Willie. Hurry. Ambulance and police," Mary shouted, pushing Willie aside to get to the man in the car.

"Can you hear me, sir?" Mary asked. She listened. "Can you hear me, sir?" She asked again. The man was unresponsive.

"Willie," Mary instructed, "go to the other side. Pull him off the steering wheel and drag him on his back across the front seats if you can."

Willie dragged, and Mary released the man's legs from the footwell until they had him on his back across the front seats.

"Lower the back of the passenger seat for me, Willie," Mary instructed as she scrambled into the back of the car.

Leaning forward awkwardly, she intuitively put her CPR training into practice. She spoke again to the man, but he was still unresponsive, She felt for his pulse but couldn't find one. Making sure his airways was clear, she gave him mouth-to-mouth, followed by chest compressions.

Willie, watching her, realised the car's engine was still running. He let it run.

Tiring, administering the mouth-to-mouth and chest compressions, beads of sweat gathering on her face, Mary was about to ask Willie to take over when she heard the man gasp. It was faint, but it was there.

"He's alive, Willie, he's alive," she yelled before returning to the man to reassure him that he was safe and help was coming. Mary wasn't sure if he could hear or understand what she was saying but bent over him; she kept whispering into his ear.

Willie moved into the back beside her out of the cold. With the engine still running, the car was warm. He sat on something hard. As Mary comforted the injured man, Willie wriggled a little box he was sitting on out from under him. He had seen it before. It was the little mahogany case their parish priest brought with him when called to administer the sacrament of the sick to Willie's dying mother. Willie thought, *it couldn't be, could it?*

"Willie, he's trying to tell me something," Mary said without looking around.

"I think I know who he is, Mary," Willie responded. Mary turned to look at Willie. "I think it's Father Fogarty. It must have been an emergency; otherwise, he wouldn't be out on a night like this. Would he? Did he say anything? We need to know where he was going."

Mary turned back to the injured man, leaning over him and whispering. The only sound in the car was the engine ticking over. Seconds ticked away; it seemed like minutes. *Response times for emergency services in this weather are out the window,* Willie told himself. *I think we will just have to wait and see.*

Mary carried on whispering in the man's ear. Slowly, Mary turned to Willie, "You're right," she said. "Father Fogarty was on his way to visit your friend Jack up at the top of the Croft Road, who is very ill. What are we going to do?"

Willie's friend Jack was at home recovering from major surgery.

"He must be bad if they're sending for the priest at this time of the night in this weather," Willie said, thoughts flicking through his mind. "You stay here with Father Fogarty. It's nice and warm. Keep the engine running; there's plenty of petrol in the tank. I'll go back to Jack's house and explain what's happened. They'll be waiting for him. Maybe they'll be able to find another priest, but I doubt it on a night like this. But at least they'll know what's happened. I won't delay. I'll be back as soon as I can."

"Why don't you just ring them? You've got your mobile?"

"Yes, I have, but it's the kind of thing I want to do in person. Okay? Will you be alright?"

Willie had battery-operated hazard warning lights in the back of the Passat he used at work when occasion demanded. He positioned them around Father Fogarty's car before heading for the sick house.

Parking at his friend's house gate, he saw the hall light coming on. *They're expecting the priest,* he thought. Jack's wife Josephine had the front door open before Willie was halfway down the garden path. Coming face to face and realising he wasn't the priest, Josephine's anguished look could not disguise her disappointment. Impulsively, Willie stepped forward and, holding Josephine tenderly in his arms, eased her into the hall and closed the front door.

Concern for the well-being of Father Fogarty occupied much of the conversation. Surrounded by Josephine and her family, he told them what had happened. As he left, Josephine told Willie, "Go in and say your goodbyes, Willie. I don't think Jack will last the rest of this night."

Willie drove back down to the Black Arch. The car was still there, ringed by red lights. Inside, Mary and the priest, as comfortable as could be in the circumstances, were talking. He told Mary what had happened.

"I was driving along slowly when I had this excruciating pain in my chest. I think I blacked out. The next thing I knew, you were talking to me."

Bells ringing in the distance announced help was near and were backed up by approaching flashing blue lights. The medics and police took over as Mary and Willie looked on. When Father Fogarty was whisked away to the hospital, only his car remained to be dealt with. It was undamaged and fit to drive. There was no other vehicle involved.

Mary drove Father Fogarty's car back to the parochial house with Willie chugging behind in the Passat. *What to do next?* They wondered. Father Fogarty lived alone. He had a housekeeper, but she didn't live in. *Ring the Bishop?* They dismissed that thought. In the end, they decided to leave everything until the morning. They had forgotten it already was morning.

"Let's go home, Mary."

"We're here now. We might as well go and see if Isobel's lights are still off."

"Are you serious?"

"We might as well now we've come this far."

Willie smiled when they saw the light in Isobel's window.

***

In bed, they mulled over the twists of fate that led them to the car slewed across the Coast Road, where they wound up saving the life of their parish priest.

"Father Fogarty should have retired long ago, you know Mary."

"I know, but it's his vocation. It's what he wants to do, Willie. My mother thought the world of him, you know. He's a real priest, she would say. When our Lord walked around the Holy Land, he must have been very like Father Fogarty."

"After tonight, Mary, I don't think he'll be able to carry on."

"You know Willie, that's the first time I've had to use the CPR training I received. Never in my wildest dreams did I think that I would find myself in a situation like that."

"Mary, you were amazing. I wouldn't have known what to do without you."

"You know Willie, I just think it was fate we were there to-night," she said, putting out the light. It's a night to remember."

An Excellent Vintage

It was mid-April, mid-morning. Two seniors were enjoying their constitutional amble. In their ninth decade, they ambled; the distances travelled shortened, and the time lengthened.

Contentedly, they strolled into the Town Park, pausing to admire the clusters of daffodils and tulips, unashamedly competing for attention, the allottees earnestly preparing beds for sowing and planting and the fruit trees mantled in snow-white blossoms. The air they breathed was bursting with expectation.

The faraway pastel blue sky was drawn closer by little lumps of white fleecy clouds slowly floating across the heavens; clouds with substance, shape, form, and colour with their distinct beauty.

Barking dogs in the distance attracted their attention, alerting them to the big white dog on the end of a long leash, limbering nonchalantly towards them, its raised wet nose earnestly sniffing their nearness. Alongside them, it was more than knee-high.

The man, on the other end of the dog's leash, reigned the dog in, smiled and said, "Don't worry; he's a big sissy. He's harmless." The he and his four-legged friend went on with their walk.

At the Bank Heads, the elderly couple paused by the granite stone wall to catch their breath and absorb once again the familiar vista that opened up before them.

Moving to the seaward side of the wall, they stood at the top of the winding path leading down to the promenade, far below them. It seemed a long way down. To their left, their destination was in plain view, unoccupied; they would have it all to themselves. Time was when they could run up and down the path with gay abandon, but not anymore.

It was almost noon. The sun high in the light blue sky above the Inver Braes beamed generously down, making them feel nice and warm. Facing southwards, partially sheltered from the light easterly breeze, the shouts of footballers in the distant Bay Field drifted up on waves of excitement—happy noises, comforting and reassuring, spoiled only by the raucous squealing of scavenging seagulls. In a tree behind them, a blackbird burst into a full-throated trilling song, inconsiderately interrupted by an intercom announcement on the P&O ferry berthed in the harbour, disturbing the pastoral ambience.

An arrogant magpie walking within touching distance, picking on the tarmacadam path for bits of anything that caught its foraging eye, encouraged them to reset and surrender to the moment again. The P&O ferry eased from its harbour mooring on an ebbing tide and sailed away on a calm bluish-green sea mirroring the colours in the sky. There was a haziness on the horizon where the sea and sky merged, a thin space the old folk would have called it. High above them, aeroplanes passing on northern and southern trajectories stained the pale blue sky with billowing vapour trails that lingered like threatening shadows at a wake.

Settled, the afternoon quietened. It was less busy. This quiet time, time to themselves, with themselves, they loved. Looking back the way they had come, the granite stone wall bent its way towards Drumalis, the stand of Sitka Spruce trees leaning seawards forming an impressive evergreen backdrop. Further down the embankment, a thicket of blackthorn bushes covered in breathtaking snowy white blossoms cheerfully announced spring and beyond the grove of tall native trees, oak, beech and horse chestnut wearied by their wintering, uncanopied, had not yet deemed its presence. Trees in all seasons appealed to their imagination. The light easterly breeze rippling gently through the naked trees against a backcloth of the blue sky created an elaborate silhouetted choreography that made them come alive. In a bush behind them, a chiffchaff raised its melodious voice in a rapidly rising riff that slowly fell and tailed away.

Max, that's his name, let his thoughts flow, taking him on a mystery tour of memory. On his way to the Town Park, football boots slung over one shoulder and a bag over the other to play in a match, he saw a figure zigzagging up the road on a bicycle, knees rising and falling like pistons furiously pumping the pedals. As the distance between them closed, he realised the figure was a girl on a man's heavy, ugly bike that was too big for her. Her curly black hair flowed from side to side in rhythm with her pumping knees. As she whizzed past, he just smiled at the absurdity of it. That was his first sight of Alice, his wife, beside him.

Two weeks later, reluctantly, he accompanied pals to the Saturday night dance in the Kings Arms hotel. Standing at the bar, which, in those faraway days he recalled, served soft drinks and ice cream, he found himself beside a girl he thought familiar. He was shy. She was friendly. Then he uttered the most ridiculous chat-up line ever, "Do you ride a man's bike?"

They didn't dance; they just talked until the dancing stopped, and he walked Alice home.

The day they married, there was ice on the roads. Spring was far off, but they were too much in love to wait for sunshine. In the back of a Volkswagen Beetle, they ventured forth to honeymoon in the hills and valleys of Wicklow, beginning their journey in life together.

One October evening, sitting enjoying a warming fire, Alice told him she was pregnant. That was an evening to cherish. Managing expectations and the enormity of the parenting challenge occupied their conversation for the rest of the evening.

Max remembered where he was and what he was doing when their firstborn left the safety of Alice's womb. Uncertain about where to go, he presented at the maternity ward with flowers and a smile. Alice was waiting, their son in her arms. The mop of black hair on the boy's head caught his eyes. It was a while before he noticed Alice's black eyes. She looked bruised, battered and utterly exhausted. Later, she would tell him how difficult the birthing was. Max suspected that was only half of the story. Walking home from the maternity ward, a father, the enormity of his responsibility fell on him like a wall of bricks.

Sitting beside Alice, Max realised how ignorant he was, how little he knew, how naive, and how ill-prepared. Human biology, he recalled, had never found expression or even a hint in his formative education. Different now, he thought, thankfully.

Birthing protocols had changed when they were expecting their fourth child; husbands could be present supporting their wives. Max remembered letting go of Alice's hand when the baby's head appeared. It was such a wonderful, joyous, extraordinary experience that he momentarily forgot about Alice. It was also a moment when his love of Alice increased exponentially, and his appreciation for women soared.

Their journey in life was not all sunshine. There were ups and downs, celebrations and disappointments—the shadow of death, always a close companion, acknowledged with age. Children grow up expecting to outlive their parents, but parents don't expect to outlive their children. Their child's unexpected, tragic loss was difficult for Max and Alice to endure, but they did. He was in his third year at university with his future before him. In his loss, they grew closer together.

Here we are, Alice; Max was thinking, in our sunset season, you and I are making the best of things and thankful for it. A couple of old plodders, we'll keep plodding on whatever comes our way, as we've always done shoulder to shoulder.

Alice remembered him walking in with his mop of thick black, unruly curly hair flopping freely over his brow when she was about to leave the library. Brushing it aside, he smiled at her in passing. She noted his eyes were brown. At least a head taller than her, he walked in a lazy, easy, athletic way that suggested contentedness within.

"Hi," he said and was gone.

Their subsequent encounter was in the Kings Arms ballroom. It was an unforgettable evening. They talked and shared lemonade and ice cream until the last dance was called just before midnight. That was how it was back then. Afterwards, he walked her home, parting with good nights exchanged and a date to spend Sunday afternoon on Islandmagee.

They didn't have a lengthy prelude to marriage; happy in themselves, they got on with it with minimal preparation and planning. Youthfully naive, they sallied forth, committed to making the best of whatever life threw at them.

She looked forward to the birth of their firstborn, but her mother hadn't prepared her in any way for the ordeal it turned out to be. She endured the birthing process alone for more than seven agonising hours. Looking in a mirror, preparing for Max's visit, she looked like she had been pulled through a hedge and flayed.

Max breezed in with eyes only for their son: his black hair, blue eyes, hands, fingers, feet and toes and the tag on one of his toes.

He was talking, talking, talking when all Alice needed was a hug.

The loneliness when Max was abroad working was hard to bear. Her days were busy with the children and their schooling, but the nights alone in bed without Max by her side were, at times, insufferable. At night, she read herself into sleep.

Max was also abroad when she nearly fainted with fright the day she saw a mouse in the house. In desperation, Alice summoned her brother and demanded he rid her of it, which he did. But the damage was done when leaving; he told her she was lucky it wasn't a rat, adding there are always rats where there are rivers. When Max got home, her bags, in her mind, were already packed in readiness for their new home, wherever that might be, as long as it wasn't close to a river. It never crossed her mind to ask how far away from a river she would need to be, to be safe from rats.

When she miscarried, she felt lost, defeated, and a failure. Max was fantastic, but she knew he didn't fully understand her feelings. She doubted any man could understand. They named their lost child Nicholas Joseph.

Much later, the tragic loss of their firstborn was difficult to bear. Max was shattered but remained functional. He avoided people and couldn't talk about their loss until the passage of time healed his wounded heart.

It was evening when Alice answered the phone. The voice in her ear offered condolences on her son's death. Alice apologised to the caller, saying, "Sorry, you've got the wrong number," ending the conversation. Max was abroad, and Alice was busy with the children and thought no more about the phone call. She didn't know her son was dead. In the hours that followed, his tragic death was confirmed. Alice crumbled but didn't fall apart; her children needed her, and she needed them. She often said, "My children and my faith saved me."

Alice knew that the time they shared, where they sat, was a sacred moment of reflection on their lives together. She glanced at Max, lost in his thoughts, her soul mate of long-standing, long-suffering. A worker, a builder of homes in more ways than Alice could enumerate. *He doesn't deserve this*, she was thinking. *I don't want to burden him. I don't want him left alone; he won't be able to cope. He needs me more at this moment than I need him. God, what are you doing? Your will be done. Amen.*

An indignant crow perched on the stone wall looked them in the eye and cawed and cawed accusingly as if they had deliberately spoiled its afternoon before flying off in disgust. The sounds of children at play in the adjacent playground signalled the end of their silent sanctuary. More people would be out walking dogs and enjoying the rest of the day.

Shuffling feet alerted them to someone approaching. Max turned to look and thought he saw the familiar flicker of insincerity slip across her face before, without pausing for a breath, she said, "Good afternoon. How are you? Isn't that a beautiful afternoon? You're looking well. Great to see you?"

Max and Alice had heard it all before, many times, moving lips, mouthing insincere words that insulted the ears and intellect of the receiver. A collector and purveyor of gossip, bits and pieces of other people's lives, good or bad; the more colourful, the better; it would be exchanged with considerable embellishment if the exchange rate was ample. Elaboration, for her, was a cultivated art form. She was like a gawker at a road traffic accident.

Alice responded elliptically, knowing that trying any diversion tactic was a waste of time. Undeterred, the gossiper continued probing for news; how were they coping? Was their family abroad all right? Would they be visiting them soon? How long would they be staying? What news of their grandchildren? How many do they have now? And much more? When the well of meaningless exchanges ran dry, she shuffled off to find other prey.

The sun was still high in the pale blue sky, the landscape hadn't changed, and the children in the playground were amusing themselves, but sometimes a moment's beauty can be tarnished.

Suddenly, the afternoon was alive with activity. Alice and Max soon were surrounded by small dogs, big dogs, leashed and unleashed, happy dogs and happy dog carers. It was a dog party to which they were the uninvited but welcome guests. It was time for Max and Alice to journey home.

It was nearing tea time when they approached the driveway that gently wound up to the front of their house. In summers past, their children raced on scooters up and down it and sometimes used it for winter sports, but that was a long time ago. Max braced himself to push Alice in her wheelchair up to their front door. It wasn't a taxing gradient, and he made short work of it.

Although mobility impaired, Alice was not yet a wheelchair user, but walking was sometimes challenging. Max had suggested they get one of the powered scooters, but independently-minded Alice was having none of it, "Not yet, Max. I'll tell you when," she responded each time he suggested it.

In the end, he left it with her. Max waited for Alice to ease herself off the wheelchair before helping her grasp the mobility handrails he had fitted at the front door two years ago. The walk into the living room was almost too much for Alice. She sank into her reclining chair, freeing Max to prepare the supper he had planned before they went out for their afternoon walk.

After supper, Alice, with Max's assistance, readied herself for bed and retired with her book.

In the kitchen, Max tidied up and grappled with unwanted, disturbing thoughts.

I'm an old man; should I be doing this?

I made breakfast, lunch and supper and washed up. I do it every day. I stripped the bed, put on new sheets and a duvet, and put the washing on the line; when I've finished here, I'll have to bring it all in, fold and stash it away.

Increasingly, I have to help Alice in the bathroom. I know she doesn't like it, and I'm not too fond of it either, but I have to do it, and I'll have to help her more often. Oh God, why does it have to be like this?

Tomorrow, I have to do a grocery shop, think about what food we'll eat in the week ahead, and reorder Alice's medication online. What a bind! I hate bloody passwords. I have a book full of the dammed things, and then I need to go to the hole in the wall to get cash. The number of times I've gone into shops and ordered something, offered my card to pay only to be informed,

"It's cash only, sir."

Once, someone took pity on me and offered to pay, but I couldn't accept. And me without a penny in my pocket. My pride got in my way.

The grass needs cutting, and there's a lot of weeding, plants to feed, hedges to trim and trees to prune. It's too much. I can't cope.

Jobs about the house I used to do, I can't do anymore, I haven't the time, I have to get someone in to do them. The plumber is coming tomorrow to fit a washer. What is happening to me?

What am I going to do? Alice's condition will not improve. What if she becomes incontinent? Will I be able to manage?

There is so much in my head; I have to make notes: bills to pay, car to MOT, tax and insurance, house insurance to see to, the intruder alarm to get serviced, the list is endless. There is so much going on. If you're outside looking in, it will all look serene, carefree and calm. How did I cope before?

Stop and think, Max.

Alice made it easy for you. Don't you see? You had your career and a job you loved. You travelled a lot. Did Alice ever complain? You were free to go and do whatever you had to. Stop whining. She raised your children almost single-handedly. Why?

Love Max. She cared for you, loved you.

Now you are her carer. Banish your negativity, Max, embrace positivity and live for the moment's joy. You are bound together, Alice to you, and you to her.

At peace with himself, Max loaded up a tray with their night-caps and joined Alice in the sanctuary of their bedroom. Later, he was preparing to return the tray to the kitchen when Alice, setting her book aside, looked at him, smiled and took his hand in hers—a benediction with understanding, imagination, and memory.

In bed in the still, quietness of the night, Alice asleep beside him, Max, gently taking her hand in his, recalled the psalmist's words:

'Now that I am old and grey,
God, do not desert me.'

Concluding his reflection, he gave thanks for the gift of another day.

Old Shoes

When brand new
dressed a window
alluring passing feet
that they might live.

Now forsaken lie
in casual disarray
childishly discarded
unwanted, unloved, abandoned.

Down at heel
scuffed and shabby
soles wafer thin
flimsy and porous.

Shoes have soles
real, authentic, tangible.
wear and tear
in plain sight.

Shoes have mouths
full of tongues.
Bereft of voice
they cannot speak.

They have memory.
Storeys to tell
about their wearers
and much more.

Bringing near distant,
places they've been
terrains traversed
pilgrimages journeyed.

Like old shoes
we have souls
delicate and permeable.
Sometimes thin souled.

Old shoes restored
feeling like new
eager and purposeful
await new challenges.

When thin souled
your journey wearisome
raise your eyes
Go and explore.

Let imagination
illuminate the way
renewed and strengthened
Soaring on eagle's wings.

The Noah's Ark Project

On board the Liverpool ferry in Belfast, his weekend bag safely stowed in his berth, Adrian settled snugly in the corner of the lounge with his drink, opened his book and began to read. The lounge was hot and noisy, everyone talking and bantering about football.

His nose buried in the book, he ignored the lounge rapidly filling with fellow Liverpool supporters on their way to Anfield, as he was, for the big game on Saturday against Arsenal.

"It's a bit busy in here. Mind if I squeeze in beside you?" A voice enquired

Glancing up from his book, he saw a stout, paddy-capped, ruddy-faced gentleman in a long black belted overcoat, full pint glass in hand, pipe in mouth, peering down at him.

"Not at all. Be my guest," Adrian responded, moving aside to make room before returning to his book.

Doors opened as passengers went onto the deck to watch the lights of Belfast recede, venting some of the cigarette smoke but not a lot. The lounge slowly filled with blue, hazy cigarette fumes billowing in waves underneath the ceiling. Thankful that his companion's pipe wasn't yet glowing, Adrian hoped it would remain that way; otherwise, he would be having an early night. The fumes would saturate his clothes, and he would taste the nicotine, but he wasn't planning on staying in the lounge long before touring the deck and retiring to his berth.

The ferry was easing out of Belfast Lough when his fellow passenger asked, "Are you interested in seafaring?" His question, prompted by the cover of Adrian's book.

Not another loquacious bore that I'm going have to endure, Adrian thought. But light-heartedly, disguising his displeasure, he answered, "Not really. My son's school project is about the port of Larne. I'm just reading up on some stuff in preparation for when he starts firing questions at me when I get back home after the match."

"Not hard to know who you support. I support Arsenal. Are you from Larne?"

"Yes." *Just my luck,* he thought, *I chose this spot to avoid company, and I end up cheek by jowl beside an Arsenal supporter who'll bend my ear all evening boasting about 'The Invincibles'. Wherever I go, some cling-on finds me.*

"I was in Larne last week for the commemoration of the Princess Victoria disaster. I know a bit about the port of Larne and have a story that might interest your son. I'll be right back. My name's Sam by the way, Sam Dolan. Same again?" he asked, pointing to Adrian's glass. He'd left for the bar before Adrian had a chance to say no.

Thinking Sam didn't take long to down that pint, Adrian was trying to figure out who Sam might be and how he might earn his living when his genial fellow passenger returned bearing drinks.

"Cheers. Yes, the story I mentioned is a true story."

Here we go again, Adrian thought, *this always happens. How do I attract them? No doubt you will feature prominently in the story.* Concealing his discomfort, Adrian unenthusiastically acknowledged the offer. "Good. Great. Thank you. I'm Adrian, Adrian Logan."

"Well, Adrian, this story starts before your time." Taking more than a sip of his Guinness, Sam sat back, holding his pipe by the unlit bowel, and launched into his story.

"In September 1939, Germany invaded Poland, forcing Great Britain and France to declare war on Germany, thus heralding the beginning of World War Two. Following the attack on Pearl Harbour in 1941, America declared war on Imperial Japan. Before that treacherous act, America provided Great Britain and her Allies with significant military supplies and other support.

"What does this have to do with this story and your son's project? Well, you might ask Adrian. Everything.

"Following the attack on Pearl Harbour, the deployment of American troops in Northern Ireland significantly increased, necessitating the construction of military bases, including naval bases. The Allies' military strategists and planners led by General Eisenhower were developing plans for an Anglo-American campaign in northwest Africa, codenamed Operation Torch in 1942 and the liberation of Europe beginning with the invasion of Normandy, codenamed Operation Neptune in 1944. These and similar operations needed vessels capable of offloading heavy vehicles onto suitable hard standings. Tank landing craft, much larger and more robust than troop landing craft, successfully fulfilled that need. These tank landing craft were ships fitted with rear ramps to allow tanks and heavily ladened lorries to self-load and unload.

"To supply the build-up of their military in Northern Ireland, the American Navy built a new dock at the north pier in the port of Larne on which tank landing craft could offload their heavy cargo. When the war ended in 1945, the fleet of tank landing craft was decommissioned and mothballed on the River Clyde.

"For me, this is where this story gets fascinating. My uncle Joey, with maritime interests and familiar with the port of Larne, would often, on his way across to Stranraer, rack his brains pondering how he could use the concrete ramp built to facilitate the tank landing craft at the north pier in Larne Harbour, to further his business interests. A germ of an idea fermenting in his mind was predicated on a connection between Larne and Preston. Joey knew that the Preston Dock on the River Ribble had a concrete ramp similar to the one in Larne Harbour. However, the scheme had two problems for which solutions were needed to make Joey's project viable. He needed financial backing and the vessels to operationalise the project.

"With connections in the maritime business, Joey sold his idea to three friends. Together, they formed a new company, Ferry Traders Ltd, to generate the freight business needed to sustain the enterprise. To make the scheme tangible, reliable service was essential. How to secure that caused Joey many sleepless nights. But fate intervened. Disembarking in Preston, Joey called on a friend, as he always did when in Preston, who happened to be a fruit and vegetable importer. Chatting, Joey sketched out his dilemma. His friend told him about a conversation with an acquaintance who had in mind what he referred to as his 'Norah's Ark' project that had something to do with reusing mothballed ships. Joey probed his friend for more information without success. With his antenna on full alert, he contacted everyone he knew in the freight transport and distribution business, searching for information on a 'Norah's Ark' project without success. But although disappointed, he was not defeated. On the point of throwing in the towel, he tried another search.

"More in hope than expectation, he telephoned a rail freight office in London and was astounded to find someone knowledgeable about the 'Norah's Ark' project. In this story, there is a string of the most unlikely tenuous connections that fortuitously occur to enable Joey Dolan's germ of a notion to succeed.

"Colonel Frank Bustard now enters the story. Frank Bustard was Passenger Manager for the White Star Line until he left to start a company that would offer ten pound fares to sail from Liverpool to New York, but his plan died the death at the outbreak of the Second World War. He was, without doubt, way ahead of his time, wanting to promote low-cost, no-frills travel. He was, in every sense, a British shipping pioneer. Colonel Bustard OBE served as an embarkation officer in the First World War and was mentioned in dispatches four times. In the Second World War, he served as part of Movement Control, including Operation Neptune and the D-Day invasion of Normandy and was mentioned twice in despatches. He was very familiar with tank landing craft and their operation. In addition, he had access to government departments that enabled him to obtain the use of the tank landing craft mothballed on the River Clyde and create the Transport Ferry Service Company. He was an exuberant, larger-than-life character who got things done. A doer, Uncle Joey often said.

"The germ fermenting in my uncle Joey's head yielded its fruit in 1948 when roll-on roll-off tracking between Larne and Preston, using modified tank landing craft, was operationalised commercially for the first time in the world. The business was slow initially; the industry, wary about new-fangled ideas, was sluggish on the uptake, but again, luck lent its helping hand.

"At the end of the Second World War, AW Hawksley began manufacturing non-traditional houses at the government's request instead of producing aircraft. Very soon, aluminium bungalows were flowing off the production line. One complete unit every fifteen minutes of every working day. Each unit, about five and a half tons in weight, had four rooms, a fitted kitchen and a bathroom, complete with plumbing and electric wiring. They were essentially aluminium framed boxes, externally clad with painted aluminium sheeting, foamed slag concrete and an inner leaf of plasterboard. The units delivered to their respective sites on purpose-built double-decker trailers were complete in every respect and ready for assembly on pre-prepared concrete raft foundations. The first shipments of aluminium bungalows for distribution in Northern Ireland used the new roll-on roll-off ferry service between Preston and Larne.

"As the roll-on roll-off ferry service attracted more business, a fleet of new vessels was needed. The Bardic Ferry, the first of the new fleet designed to carry a mix of 69 commercial vehicles and 13 cars came into service in 1957. The rest is history, as they say. The Larne service switched from Preston to Cairnryan, ownership of the service changed too, and the port of Larne built new roll-on roll-off tracking docks."

Sam, his story told, sat back, chewing on the stem of his empty pipe, and waited for Adrian's reaction. He was surprised when Adrian said, "You know, Sam, that's not the whole story. There's a lot more."

Sam didn't know that Adrian was born and reared in an aluminium bungalow beside Dixon Park in Larne and that his father was still happily living there. Adrian, forgetting about the cigarette smoke lingering overhead, regaled Joe for the next hour with stories of growing up in a colony of aluminium bungalows that had a fifteen-year life expectancy when they were erected in 1948 and were still much loved by their occupants in 2023.

When they parted to go their separate ways, the best of friends, Adrian, in his berth, reflected on his misjudgement of

Sam when he squeezed in to sit beside him. Sam wasn't dull but engaging, entertaining, charming and knowledgeable. He was the opposite of everything Adrian had thought he would be. "Let that be a lesson to you, Adrian," he told himself, switching off the light.

That's the story my dad told me when he returned from Liverpool. He wasn't in the best form. Arsenal beat Liverpool 2-0 to win the league, but he eventually got over it.

I thought he would draft something for me to copy. He didn't.

"Write your own story your way," he said. "Colour it in your own words, and it will be authentic."

I wrote my story. It wasn't very long. I got good grades but, more importantly, words of encouragement that shaped my future. I never met genial, big-hearted Sam, but I am forever in his debt.

Aspiration

I want to grow
Like an Oak tree
Anchored tall and sturdy
Stretching heavenwards
My majestic canopy
Mantling many manors

Creating habitations
For native species
Welcoming seasonal migrants
With heartening sustenance
My skin graffiti scratched
With love tokens

Filled with gratitude
Looking upwards
Sustained by the wonder
Of my maturing
Surprised by my longevity.

But what is time?
Other than a metric of imagination

New Beginnings

He sat, hunched in the corner of the front room of his home in Carson Street, staring furtively out the Venetian screened window, a telephone thrust against his ear, anxiously listening to a distant, unfamiliar ring tone. Suddenly, a crisp voice spoke in a language Vinnie didn't understand. Confused, he didn't respond. The voice repeated itself. This time, Vinnie answered.

"Father Fergus? Is he there?"

"Who shall I say is calling?" A cultured English voice asked.

"Me, he'll know it's me," Vinnie retorted, frustration edging his response.

"Hold while I see if he can take your call."

Shrinking further into the corner, Vinnie waited, the telephone glued to his ear as if his life depended on it. He was the younger of two brothers, prone to mischief in his brother's absence. Suddenly, the voice he wanted to hear was in his ear.

"Fergus here."

"It's a long time since you heard my first confession, Fergus."

"Vincent, how are you?"

"Okay, Fergus, and you?"

"Not bad, Vincent, not bad at all. But what about you?"

"It's two years since Covid took Fiona, Fergus. I thought I was coping, but it's difficult and getting harder. I need to talk. Can I come and see you?"

"Anytime, Vincent, you know that. You don't have to ask."

"Are you sure?"

"Of course, I'm sure. Come when you want and don't worry about accommodation, you can crash with me. How's that?"

"Great."

"Vincent, I have to dash now, I have classes. Ring me to let me know when you are coming. Okay?"

"I will," he said, relief flushing through him, ending the call.

Not long after graduating from university, Vinnie met Fiona. Eighteen months later, they married and set up a home on Carson Street, dearly wanting to start a family. A decade later, they were childless. But they didn't give up hope. In 2020, Fiona had a hospital appointment for another routine infertility procedure. She made sure the house was tidy before they left to go to the hospital and gently admonished Vinnie, saying, "Keep it that way, Vinnie. I'll only be in the hospital overnight."

Entering the hospital, he noticed the shiny, clean floors and a lingering vague sickness smell tinted with disinfectant. But it wasn't routine. Fiona's overnight stay became two nights, then three nights.

On the fourth night, he found her in a different ward with tubes in her nose, feeding her oxygen. She seemed okay, a little breathless. Fiona, an asthmatic child, had grown out of it. Slowly, her condition improved, raising Vinnie's hopes that she would soon be home.

On what was to be her eighth night in hospital, Vinnie took a phone call at work. Fiona's condition suddenly worsened, and they put her on a ventilator. Rushing to the hospital, he found Fiona in intensive care, an oxygen mask covering her face. She smiled weakly up at him. As soon as he set eyes on her, he feared the worst. From behind a screen, he watched a tube feed put down her throat; Fiona slipped into an induced coma. Vinnie, rooted to the spot, knew it was serious, life or death, a toss of a coin, which way it would go. Fiona's life, a toss of a coin? His mind was a whirlpool of confusion.

Days became weeks. Weeks became months. When the phone by his bedside rang at 5.37 a.m., he knew what the shrill noise signalled. Driving like someone demented, ignoring speed limits, Vinnie was at the hospital without delay. He was almost too late. The light of life was slipping away from her eyes, but Vinnie could see Fiona knew him and was aware of what was happening. She knew, he knew, too. The sorrow of her great helplessness sucked Vinnie down into a suffocating quagmire. Tears leapt into his eyes. When he opened them, Fiona was gone. Her life's thread severed; she floated away. Dazed, he thought, she looked so lovely and peaceful. Later, despairingly, he would be thankful they were childless.

The medical staff stood by. There was nothing anyone could do. The bed was in demand. Not a word was spoken. And Vinnie, like all those around him, was utterly helpless. Then, they screened her remains. It was a raw red wound for which there wasn't and wouldn't be any relief for a long time. He just had to stand there stunned and bear it like a man. Vinnie wondered if he had any faith.

He had taken her to the hospital for a routine procedure because she wanted to be a mother. A hospital, a safe place, was giving him back a lifeless body. Absurdly, he wondered what he was supposed to do with it. Nothing would be going home with Vinnie other than excruciating grief. Fiona had often said a lifeless body is like a soul without grace. Something wasn't adding up. Fiona contracted Covid-19 in the hospital. It just didn't make sense. But then, it was early days, not yet epidemic or pandemic.

Fiona's funeral was a solemn, dreary affair. There were a handful of social-distanced mourners. Vinnie sat alone. He didn't remember or want to remember anything about it. When the sliding doors opened like gaping jaws, and her coffin rolled towards the ominous intimacy of the crematorium, Vinnie lifted his head, trying to pray, petitioning for purgatory at least.

Back home, he closed the door to the world and sat in the neat and tidy front room, laughing almost hysterically at the irony of it, thinking, *I kept it neat and tidy for you, Fiona, didn't I?* Then his dam of bitter tears burst.

Days passed, he drifted in grief, and the pandemic arrived. He watched government ministers doing their televised public briefings. They made him feel so sick that he wanted to spew his guts out like a splatter gun all around the spick and span living room Fiona had left when she entered the hospital.

Slowly stripped of everything good in his life, Vinnie withdrew into himself, his inner darkness, only leaving the shelter of the house for work. He stopped going to church. No one noticed. A crust calcified on the surface of his soul, leaving little room for grace, letting nothing in or out.

An insatiable depression seeded in him and grew like a rampant weed draining his will to live. Part of him wished he were dead.

"What have I to live for?"

He would torment himself with the same question over and over again. He couldn't talk to anyone or tell anyone his problem; he didn't know himself, so how could he tell anyone? Everyone knows anyway. Yet he knew they couldn't understand what he was thinking or feeling. Everyone around him was as helpless as he was.

Lying in bed one evening, Vinnie sought to come to terms with the imaginings in his mind. The room was dark and quiet. It was weird; he was surrounded by cheerful, happy people, at peace with themselves, while he writhed secretly in an agony that would not ease. It made him feel contemptuous of everyone around him. Vinnie felt the shadow of death enter, pause and pass through. He had seen it in Fiona's eyes. It wasn't his time yet; death was telling him. That was the moment he decided to reach out to Father Fergus.

After nearly three weeks of soul searching, Vinnie was going via Dublin airport to meet Father Fergus in Rome. He had tried unsuccessfully to contact him on the Saturday morning he left home, but left a message on an answering machine that included his flight number and arrival time at Leonardo Da Vinci airport and naively thinking no more about it, set off on his way to Rome.

Disembarking, he passed quickly through passport control and made his way to the terminal exit, expecting Father Fergus to be waiting for him. He wasn't there. Vinnie checked his mobile phone for a message. There was none. He searched for a pickup point and found it. Father Fergus wasn't there. Vinnie wondered if Father Fergus hadn't gotten his message or maybe he was ill. The wait lengthened, Rome's day shortened, and Vinnie's anxiety heightened.

At the taxi rank, Vinnie fumbled in his pockets for his wallet but couldn't find it. Desperately, he searched his carry-on bag. It wasn't there. Friends warned him about airport pickpockets; he had some Euros in an inside zipped pocket, enough he hoped to get him by taxi to the Irish College.

The taxi whizzing through the streets of Rome rendered Vinnie's street map redundant. When he saw the Colosseum looming, he knew that the Irish College was not far away. Dispatching the taxi, Vinnie turned, looked at the impressive porticoed façade and made his way up the stone steps to the entrance.

In the foyer, his gaze settled on the magnificent marble stairs reaching up to a landing, from which two side stairs sprung up from either side to a higher level somewhere above his head out of sight. All this, his eyes registered through the naturally lit stairwell.

He lowered his eyes step by step to the foyer floor and noticed the stairs descending either side of the main stair to a lower level. For an absurd moment, he felt afloat in Dante's Devine Comedy, hoping he was, at worst, in limbo. He recalled that the seven terraces in Dante's purgatory represented the seven deadly sins and that the fourth terrace to negotiate was sloth and zeal, the opposite of which was virtue; blessed are those who mourn for they will be comforted. Dante, awakening from a dream, is visited by the Angel of Zeal, who removes another of the "P's", signifying sin, from his brow, thus freeing him to move up onto the fifth terrace. The recollection underpinning Vinnie's wavering hope compelled him to confront the possibility that he was wallowing in self-pity in his self-imposed purgatory.

Grappling with the thoughts cascading around in his head, he didn't hear the young man approach and ask for the third time, "Can I help you, sir?"

"Sorry, I was miles away. What did you say?"

"Can I help you, Sir?"

"Yes, please. I'm here to meet Father Fergus."

"Father Fergus?"

"Yes, Father Fergus."

"Is he expecting you?"

"Yes, he was to meet me at the airport, but I guess something came up that he had to deal with. So I made my way here."

"Have you come far?"

"From Ireland. Northern Ireland, to be precise."

"You're Irish?"

"Well, yes and no, if that makes any sense."

After a slight hesitation, The young man invited Vinnie to follow him to a small anteroom and asked him to sit and wait. On the wall opposite Vinnie was a picture of the world, suspended in space by a thread secured to something beyond the boundaries of the image, inviting the viewer's imagination.

"That sums me up," Vinnie told himself. "I'm hanging on by a thread of hope Fiona holds. She is my anchor. She doesn't want me to feel sorry for myself. Why didn't I see this before?"

Ushered into an adjoining room, Vinnie saw a priest rising to greet him from behind a vast desk littered with papers. He was a tall, lean, broad-shouldered man with a mop of black curly hair, tainted white here and there. Smiling, extending his hand, he said, "I'm Father Seamus Lavery, the Rector here for my sins. I'm Donegal, born and bred. Where are you from? Michael here tells me we're from the same neck of the woods," he said, nodding to the young man.

"I'm Vinnie, a neighbour, you might say. I'm Antrim born and bred."

Looking at Vinnie intently, he asked, "And you're looking for Father Fergus?"

"I am, yes."

"May I ask what for?"

"Sorry, Father, it's private, personal, family matters."

"Oh!"

"A family matter, Father."

"Have you known Father Fergus long?"

"Oh, yes, a long time. He heard my first confession, you know."

"Really, and you've kept in touch, have you?"

"Yes, on and off, you know."

"But what brings you here now?"

"I'd arranged to meet with Father Fergus to talk about some things."

"When did you make these arrangements?"

"About three weeks ago."

"Any contact since then?"

It was beginning to feel like an interrogation to Vinnie.

"No… No need to. It was all arranged. He told me to come anytime and not to bother about accommodation, he'd arrange everything. He said he'd pick me up at the airport, and here I am."

"Oh."

Silence thickened, filling the space between them. Vinnie sensed Father Laverty was looking for a way to tell him something he would prefer to withhold. Leaning forward in a confessional posture, hands clasped together; forefingers pressed together against pursed lips, Father Lavery raised his head and looked straight at Vinnie, saying quietly with some regret, "Father Fergus is not here… we don't know where he is. I was hoping that you…"

"What?"

"He left here without saying where he was going. We have no idea why, or where he is. I was hoping you might have some clue as to his whereabouts and why he left?"

"What? He said he would meet me. I don't understand?"

"You have no idea what has happened to him?"

"What do you think I'm doing here? My wallet was stolen at the airport. I'm short of cash. My mobile needs recharging. I've nowhere to stay. What am I supposed to do?" Vinnie's little flimsy thread of hope had snapped; his shoulders sagged, and he slumped down in his chair, a beaten man.

"You're tired, Vinnie," he heard Father Lavery say from a distance. "Let's go and have something to eat, and we can talk some more if you want to."

Father Lavery eased Vinnie onto his feet with a firm hand under Vinnie's elbow and ushered him to a small table.

"Michael is one of our seminarians, a great friend of Father Fergus," he said, introducing the young man Vinnie had already encountered. "Tea, coffee, Vinnie? Help yourself," he said, gesturing to the spread of sandwiches and food on the table that Michael had organized.

"You had your wallet stolen, Vinnie. Unfortunately, an all too frequent occurrence here," he continued, but you have your boarding pass for your return flight and your passport?"

Vinnie nodded.

"So all is not lost then, good. Here is what I suggest. I will assign Michael to assist you for the duration of your stay. Which was for three nights, I think you said. If you need anything, ask Michael. Okay? Good. Father Fergus's room is available. You can have it. You can also use the refectory for your meals at no cost. Michael will fill you in on all the details. And provide you with cash, which I must ask that you reimburse when convenient. Is that fair enough? Good. All I ask of you is that if you have any contact with Father Fergus, you ask him to contact me immediately. Please. Now I've talked enough. Let's eat."

Vinnie was very tired and hungry, and it showed. Eating slowly, he tried to marshal his confused thoughts. Father Lavery, initially his interrogator, had somehow become his friend, and it was clear that Father Fergus had left the College without confiding in Father Lavery for whatever reason. *Why didn't he tell me? Was it a sudden, spur-of-the-moment decision? It must have been, but why didn't he tell me?*

Father Lavery interrupted Vinnie's musings. "Vinnie, you look exhausted. Perhaps you should rest. We can talk tomorrow, if you want?"

"Sir…"

"Vinnie, let's dispense with the formalities. Call me Seamus, okay?"

"Okay, Seamus," Vinnie began timidly. "I was less than candid when I told you my business with Father Fergus was personal and private. I can't remember what I said. It was the truth, not the whole truth. My wife, Fiona died two years ago, and I have been having difficulties coping with her loss. That's why I was coming to see Father Fergus. I needed his help. Father Fergus is my brother, a good priest, and now he's missing."

"I saw the likeness, Vinnie, the moment I set eyes on you, and you're right; Father Fergus is an excellent priest. Let's go into my study and talk. Michael will join us later."

They talked. Vinnie did most of the talking, and Father Lavery listened.

"It's two years since Fiona died. We weren't blessed with children. People don't understand. They say silly things, stupid things. I don't talk to anyone about it. It's pointless. I'm a private person. Fiona understood that. She is with me every moment of the day and night. Everywhere I go, she is with me; I feel her presence. The piercing sting of death is now a slow-burning ache of loss that never goes away. I don't want it to go away. It's like an insatiable wound that keeps hurting, and I want it to keep hurting more and more. I owe her at least that. Don't I?"

"Vinnie, look at it this way. Your grief is a thread that needs pulling if you are to set your heart free. You told me that you and Fiona had been to Rome three or four times before. Has it not crossed your mind that perhaps Fiona has brought you back to Rome? Think about it. Father Fergus isn't here; maybe that's fortuitous. I'm here if you need me. Okay? Why don't you revisit some places you visited with Fiona?"

Vinnie's purpose in coming to Rome was to seek brotherly counselling, but now another reason materialized. *Fiona must be praying for me,* he thought. *Why not?* He believed in communion with the saints in heaven. How many times had Fiona told him that graces flowed through the prayers of others? At that moment, he felt the ache of grief easing a little. Just a touch. Was Fiona freeing him?

Early the following morning, guidebook in hand, Vinnie ventured out into a bustling Rome with a hint of a spring in his step. He was going to explore the birthplace of Rome, The Palatine. It was the first place he and Fiona visited on their honeymoon. Sauntering up, approaching the crest, the unfolding panoramic of Rome releasing his memories, Vinnie was without intent a pilgrim seeking interior peace. It was early morning, shafts of sunlight, slanting through the downy, drifting clouds, dappled the Forum.

From the bottom of the Palatine, he crossed over to the church of Saints Cosmas and Damian. Inside, beneath the Apse where he and Fiona had stood, he looked up at the great mosaic of Christ descending out of a dark blue sky on a carpet of brightly coloured clouds to present the Saints with their crowns of martyrdom. He was primarily interested in the architecture and the artistry of everything in Rome; Fiona searched for meaning and spiritual uplifting.

Now gazing up at the fresco of the descending Christ, Vinnie was spellbound. It was full of spiritual energy, sincerity and supremacy beyond his understanding. Its vigour, simplicity and solemnity gripped him. He didn't see the coronation of the martyrs; Vinnie saw Christ reaching down to him. He let his thoughts dwelt there for a long time.

It was a short walk to the Basilica di San Pietro. Vinnie had gone to admire Michelangelo's statue of Moses but now needed more than the artistry of a funeral monument. Fiona was attracted to the reliquary containing the chains used to securely bind Saint Peter whilst in prison in Jerusalem.

The crude, long-linked, heavy chains draped like a hammock awaiting a body, were displayed in a glass-fronted reliquary. Vinnie thought *there was no rest for Saint Peter wrapped in those chains; his chains were heavier than my self-imposed lighter, cruel, cutting chains.* He had begun to pray again without noticing, not vocalizing or imagining but with his heart and soul. Before the shrine, a feeling others were praying for him filled his heart.

"Time doesn't come our way twice, Vinnie; let's not waste it," Fiona often said when uncertainty clouded his judgement.

Time eased away. It was early afternoon; he hadn't eaten lunch and wasn't hungry. He would eat later in their favourite place if it were still there and he could find it. Unhurriedly on his journey of rediscovery, he travelled across the Esquiline to the Basilica di Santa Maria Maggiore. Fiona had taken him there. Vinnie walked in Fiona's footsteps to the underground Chapel of the Nativity.

There he stood before the first nativity scene created in the 13th century, the first in history, not just a depiction of an episode in Christ's life: his birth; a nativity scene in the setting it is known today. The enthroned marble statue of the Virgin Mary holding the baby Jesus on her lap with Joseph proudly standing by her right and two of the three Magi standing on her left, the third kneeling in adoration. A cow and a donkey placed slightly behind Joseph complete the tableau.

We were on our honeymoon, Vinnie thought. *I was thinking about the Emperors, history, architecture, art, the Forum and the Colosseum and many other things; Fiona had different things on her mind.'*

Next, he stood beside Fiona before the shrine of the Holy Crib, which held pieces of ancient wood that were part of the manger in which baby Jesus slept. He was restless. Fiona was transfixed.

Fiona led the way to the icon of the Virgin Mary holding the baby Jesus in her arms, which Saint Luke allegedly created. The Virgin gazes at the viewers; baby Jesus blesses the spectators with his right hand while holding a book in his left. The Virgin's hands rest protectively over baby Jesus' lap.

Now, nearly two decades after their honeymoon in Rome, Vinnie realized what it meant for Fiona to visit and petition at these shrines. Her focus was on family, the family they never had. In contrast, he was there to reconstruct the ancient city of Rome in his mind, capture the atmosphere, search the museums, and admire the art. Now, he was on catch-up, the great shrines of Rome, speaking to him, taking him to the roots of his belief.

In a childlike posture before the icon, his desire to pray intensified. He fervently prayed the Angelic Salutation three times, as he used to do before his religious beliefs had loosened and practices slackened.

He left the Basilica with a lighter step. The day had moved on without waiting for him, Vinnie realized. There was a place he wanted to visit at the Vatican, but it was late, and it was too far to walk. On his way back to the Irish College in a quiet little piazza, Vinnie sat under an awning eating his spaghetti carbonara, enjoying a glass of wine and tasting the joy of a mantling inner peace. He had begun the day without morning prayers, lost and broken, but now cleansing contrition swept through him with such pain that it almost reduced him to tears.

Later, he sat in Father Fergus's room as daylight faded. The College was quiet, the room was quiet, and Vinnie was calm in his inner self. It was night; it seemed that Fiona was suddenly beside him, her presence vivid, lifelike and heartening. Then she drifted away.

He put the light on and surveyed Father Fergus's room. It was sparsely furnished; the little altar in front of the window with the crucifix above it and the kneeler in front took his eye. He imagined his brother in prayer there. A sudden insight into the misery of his soul overwhelmed him. Extinguishing the light, he went to the altar and prayed the rosary as best he could remember.

In that zone of uncertainty between the realms of sleep, Fiona's calm voice urged Vinnie to release her, let her go, free himself and be in communion with her and all the faithful departed.

Opening his eyes to greet the dawn the following day, he felt refreshed and at peace in himself. He prayed his mother's mantra: *Be thankful for the day and all that's in it.* Then Vinnie opened Father Fergus's breviary, found the day's mass and read the liturgy of the word. Two lines galvanized his attention; *He does not break the crushed reed nor quench the wavering flame.* Meditating on those few words, Vinnie found a way back to the foundations of his belief on which to build again. He was uplifted.

An hour later, over coffee in the refectory, he revised his plans for the day ahead; he would spend the day in Trastevere as he did with Fiona on their honeymoon.

Midway across Ponte Garibaldi, he paused, looking under the bright sun down into the river Tiber, recalling how with childlike enthusiasm he had recited the stanzas of Lord Macauley's poem 'Horatio At The Bridge' for Fiona:

Then out spake brave Horatius,

The Captin of the gate:

"To every man upon this earth

Death cometh soon or late.

And how can man die better

Than facing fearful odds

For the ashes of his fathers

And the temples of his Gods."

Passersby good-naturedly applauded his performance; it was plain to them that Vinnie had a sincere tendresse for Fiona. His mind fixed on two lines in the following stanza:

"And for the holy maidens

Who feed the eternal flame."

Knowing the time for mass, Vinnie made his way quickly to the Basilica di Santa Maria in Trastevere, which Fiona had informed him was the first church in Rome dedicated to the Virgin Mary. She had taken him there specially to pray for his mother, Marian, who was seriously ill. He was like a dog on a leash as Fiona led him from one shrine to another, lighting candles and petitioning on high for his mother's wellbeing.

Now, in the Basilica waiting for mass, his mother, father, and Fiona passed on, he didn't feel alone or at a loss. He felt connected to them in an honest, meaningful, uplifting way. *"Be thankful, son, for the day and all that's in it,"* he could hear his mother say. Then the bell rang, and mass began.

After the blessing and dismissal, Vinnie sat quietly, letting the leaves of memory kindle, grateful for graces bestowed by the weight of other's prayers. Leaving the Basilica, a sign on a confessional signifying that confession was available for English speakers beckoned him. Vinnie hesitated, then decided to unburden himself, knelt in prayerful preparation and entered the confessional.

His confession was forthright, candid and authentic. It was painfully honest. Vinnie confessed that he had allowed his grief over the death of Fiona to alienate him from Jesus. He had let his soul become a spiritual desert, desiccated in the urn of self-pity. When he had finished his confession, absolution bestowed, and penance dispensed, his confessor, in parting, said, "Remember God is love. Pure love. With His grace, we can share selfless love wherever we journey."

Vinnie floated out of the Basilica from the confessional, his soul a spiritual well overflowing with grace. He hadn't noticed the morning passing; the angelus bells ringing told him it was time for lunch. Vinnie had lunch in a little quiet piazza not far from the Basilica while deciding which route to take to his next port of call. It was an off-the-tourist track, little L-shaped street that he and Fiona had happened on while wandering around Trastevere. Fiona loved it; the doors and windows of the dwellings festooned with bounteous rainbowed coloured bougainvillaeas. It was a breathtaking sight. The thing that caught Fiona's eye was the house with the blue door garlanded with red bougainvillaea. Later, in the piazza, where artists offer their wares, Fiona bought a painting of the blue door.

After lunch, quietness descended around the area. It took Vinnie quite a while to find the little street and the blue door, but eventually, he did and was not disappointed. Standing in the fragrant bougainvillaea-adorned narrow street filled with a blend of beguiling aromas, Vinnie felt the touch of Fiona's hand. It was so real he acknowledged her presence with a smile.

As Vinnie wandered around, evening descending, Trastevere became a different place. It was lively, colourful, energetic and charged with an infectious festive jubilance. Searching memory, he found the piazza where they spent their last evening. Around them, a celebration had unfolded. Musicians played, people danced and sang, and before they realized what was happening, Fiona and Vinnie were swept up and away into the very heart of it. In every respect, it was an unforgettable evening. It was the christening celebration for a young couple's first child.

Is she still here, he wondered, knowing he wouldn't recognize her if she were. *The infectious joy of that spontaneous christening celebration can never be replicated,* he thought; *nothing stands still; everything changes one way and another with time.*

Crossing Ponte Palatino to the Irish College, Vinnie paused, looked across the Tiber at Trastevere and loudly spoke:

But fiercely ran the current,

Swollen high by months of rain;

And fast his blood was flowing,

And he was sore with pain,

And heavy was his armour,

And spent with changing blows;

And oft they thought him sinking,

But still, again, he rose.

I know the feeling, he thought, moving on.

That night, he used his brother's breviary to help him pray. In the morning, he would leave Rome to return home with much to be thankful for.

After breakfast, he met with Father Lavery. Vinnie outlined how he had used his time in Rome and the healing effects he was experiencing. Father Lavery saw that this Vinnie was very different from the one he first encountered. *He's like his brother,* he thought, *mercurial.* Then Vinnie surprised him by saying, "I think I know where my brother might be."

"Do you, Vinnie? Where?"

"Well, it's a feeling, that's all mind. Fergus could be waiting for me when I get home, or he could be at our mother's old home place up the country."

"You think so?"

"I do."

"What are the chances, do you think?"

"Good is all I can say. I will tell you if I find Fergus and promise to try to convince him to talk to you. If there is anything else you think I can do, tell me, please?"

"Thank you, Vinnie. I can't ask for anything more. Your brother is an excellent priest. We all have hiccups. I don't want to lose him." Parting, he held Vinnie by the shoulders at arm's length, looked him in the eyes and said, "Cherish the love that you and Fiona shared. True love does not burn out, its everlasting flame purifies. It does not imprison you, rather, it sets you free to share the love with everyone."

Vinnie arrived home late in the evening. The house in darkness felt cold and uninhabited. His brother hadn't been there; that was clear. Vinnie's thoughts turned to the one-hundred-and-forty-plus mile drive to his mother's home in the west.

The long drive, made more bearable by the road improvements since his last excursion west, gave Vinnie time to gather his thoughts. The journey's final stretch was on a narrow road that was a mere cattle track when he was a boy. He could smell and hear the sound of the sea before he could see it. From the brow of a small hill, the end of the road in sight, he free-wheeled down, looking out over the incoming tide, and parked the car. His mother's home place off to his right was only reachable on foot. He could see the red-tiled roof of the cottage some distance away through the copse of trees, the whiff of smoke licking the chimney pot and taste the unmistakable smell of burning turf. Someone was at home.

All sorts of thoughts paraded across the frontiers of his mind. Nostalgia he pushed aside; he was here on business, serious business. It was in every respect his lane of memories. He walked between brambled hedges along the cartwheel-rutted track, his feet cushioned by the deep mossy grass. The little humble stone-built cottage with a lean-to on the side, peat smoke scenting the air, beckoned him. Anxiously approaching the solid door, Vinnie couldn't help noticing that it and the two front windows needed repainting.

The door, it seemed, sprung open to his knock. Though not unexpected, Vinnie couldn't but be surprised to see his brother standing before him, clear-eyed with healthy coloured cheeks, looking fit and well.

"Vinnie, great to see you; I've been expecting you. Come in, come in, I've got the kettle on the hob."

"What?"

"Come in, man and sit down. Michael told me all about the goings on."

"What? Michael?"

Seated around the inglenook, with evening closing in, Fergus fed the fire with turf as they talked.

It transpired that anxiety, concern and confusion had led them to their mother's home place. Vinnie's phone calls had preyed on Fergus's mind. A mind that, at the time, was experiencing what might be called a crisis of conscience. Fergus, on the spur of the moment, concluding that Vinnie's need was more urgent than his, determined to go to his brother's aid. Their corresponding flights may have passed each other somewhere over the Alps. Michael had kept Fergus abreast of what Vinnie was doing in Rome, and that Vinnie thought he knew where Fergus might be. So Fergus had waited for him.

"That's the story, Vinnie—a bit of a mix-up."

"I was in a dark place, Fergus. Rome was good for me, Fiona walked with me, and my mind fog lifted. Coming here, being with you in this place, where we were so happy, I am indebted. But what about you?"

"I'm indebted too, Vinnie, and happy for you. You have much to give to others, Vinnie."

"Fergus, I'm not stupid. There's stuff you're not telling me."

"Okay."

Fergus wasn't happy teaching in Rome. He was academically qualified; otherwise, he wouldn't be there, but he didn't want to be a professor.

"If that's what I wanted, I could have got a job in a university at home," he told Vinnie. The piazza coffee-drinking lifestyle wasn't to his taste; it didn't offer enough challenges. In essence, it was not the pastoral apostolate he had envisaged.

"In this place, mother's home place, my vocation was seeded, Vinnie. I want to be among ordinary people, the workers, the poor and the marginalized, an apostolate of the living word, evangelizing by example. I want to be a pastoral priest, caring for and supporting people in a rapidly changing world that relentlessly challenges our penny-catechism-based faith. Do you know how many pages there are in the new Catholic catechism? No? Nine hundreds and six. By listening, encouraging, fostering, and enabling discipleship, I want to build community inside and outside church walls with meaningful outreach projects. In Rome, clerical careerism is rampant. I don't want to be any part of that. When the Lord appointed the seventy-two to go out ahead of him, he said to them, *The harvest is rich, but the labourers are few, so ask the Lord of the harvest to send labourers to His harvest.* The harvest is rich today, Vinnie. People are confused, disenchanted, and hungry for knowledge and leadership. I want to be one of the Lord's labourers harvesting for Him."

"That's what makes a saint, helping the helpless."

"I don't want to be a saint."

"Don't you? Isn't that what we are all supposed to aspire to."

"Oh, come on, Vinnie, you know what I mean."

"Leaving without telling Father Lavery was a mistake, Fergus."

"I know, but I had some free time. I'm not neglecting my responsibilities, Vinnie. I thought coming and seeing you was a good idea at the time. I told Michael what I was doing. Now I realize I should have told the Rector. That was a mistake. But the time I have spent here has helped me enormously. I want to be a pastoral priest, Vinnie, and it would, I suspect, enhance my academic pursuits."

"You're a good priest, Fergus; you've found your way as I found mine. You have a good friend in Father Lavery. Trust him. At your altar, I prayed the words our mother taught us before I left:

> I waited, I waited for the Lord,
> Now at last he has stooped down to me
> and he heard my cry for help.

He has put a new song into my mouth,
a song of praise to our God;

You who wanted no sacrifice or oblation,
opened my ear.
You asked no holocaust or sacrifice for sin.
then I said, 'Here I am! I am coming!'

"I prayed, here I am, Lord, I come to do your will."

"Here we are, Lord! We come to do your will," Father Fergus responded.

Reconciled to their new beginnings, the brothers talked long into the night. With hearts wide open in the morning, they embraced and went their separate ways. The brambled hedges along the track were full of life, birds, insects and rodents; high up on a lone sycamore tree, a blackbird sang their new beginnings.

Damaged Beauty

A piddling misunderstanding
ignited and flared
into argument,
raging around them
like wildfire,
smouldering embers
marking its passing.

Damaged beauty
forlornly promenading,
together at distance,
mutual in disrespect,
muted in togetherness
lest more hurt
be unintentionally inflicted.

Naked hands flirt
flesh on flesh
fingers of feelings
brushing and touching
in language unspoken
tentatively ease open
channels of affection.

Droplets of love
fluent in tears
making a river
fill their emptiness
healing their wounds
restoring damaged beauty
dawning new beginnings.

The One That Got Away

The winter of 1963, folk said, was the worst in living memory. Thundering sleighs hurtled down the Mill Brae far into the New Year before April eventually welcomed the arrival of spring. It was hard on Wee Daft Dicky's aged mother. Going out was impossible; her arthritis flared with increasing frequency and intensity. Most of the time, she was like a creaking wheel constantly demanding attention. It was a challenging station for Richard, her son, who was always at her beck and call, 24/7. She always addressed him as Richard. Dicky, the kind-hearted soul he was, did everything he could to make his mother comfortable and content. But the more lubrication he applied, the more the creaking wheel demanded.

Christmas lunch in 1963 was a miserable affair. The slacked-up fire glowed glumly low in the Devon grate as they eked out the remains of their coal. The cold, sparsely furnished front room was cheerless. In neighbours' windows, fairy lights twinkled festive greetings. Their window onto the Brae was, by contrast, dull and gloomy. Christmas lunch was cheerless, too. It wasn't by any stretch of the imagination a feast. But tinned spam, spuds and turnip with stewed apples as a dessert was all unemployed Dicky could afford.

After lunch, sitting huddled with his mother around the pitiful fire, sparingly adding pieces of coal bit by bit, Dicky resolved that come what may, Christmas lunch next year would be a feast his mother would never forget. He reasoned that a turkey would be too much for the two of them, but a delicious roast chicken with all the trimmings would please his mother. There was more, as there always was, festering in Wee Daft Dicky's mind. He thought it would be a challenge, fun and cost-effective to rear the chicken himself. That would add value to his mother's Christmas present next year.

Those aware of Wee Daft Dicky's exploits will know he earned his nickname after a series of unfortunate mishaps in ventures pursued with good intent. His home was a small two-bedroom, kitchen terraced house with access to a right of way at the rear. The right of way was called the 'Bac's' by children using it as a playground. He and his mother lived halfway up or down, depending on how one looks at the Mill Brae. An outside lavatory and small shed reduced the width of their five-yard-long backyard to one and a half yards.

The 'Head of the Town' had a surfeit of pigeon fanciers. Every other house on the Mill Brae seemed to have a pigeon loft, out the back, somewhere. Across Magill's backfield, up and down Kitcheners Avenue, it was the same story as it was in Albert Street, Rugby Terrace, Carson Street and all around the area. They were everywhere, in all shapes and sizes. Pigeon fancying was the working man's opium.

The pigeon club in Mehaffey's Hall in Carson Street had to be swept clean after the race on Saturdays to prepare for the dance later in the evening. Before the beginning of the pigeon racing season in May, the sky around the Head of the Town would be filled mornings and evenings with swirling flocks of pigeons in training for the season to come. Sometimes, pigeons from different lofts would merge in flight in the evenings, flocking as starlings do in murmurations.

To have a plump roasted chicken to present to his mother for Christmas lunch, Wee Daft Dicky didn't intend to sit on eggs like a brooding hen. He wasn't that daft. Fairburn's had a hatchery on Coastguard Road, down at the harbour. They supplied chicken farmers with three-day-old chicks to rear, and distributed them to outlets nationwide. Wee Daft Dicky had done his research. He knew a man, who knew a man, who worked in Fairburn's, who could get him three-day-old chicks at the right price.

Wee Daft Dicky knowing nothing about chickens other than the ones he saw hung up in the butcher's window, was clueless when asked what kind of chicks he wanted. Whether they laid brown or white eggs didn't interest him; all he needed to know was that they produced good meat.

The man he knew, who knew a man, who knew about chickens, brought Wee Daft Dicky one of Fairburn's coloured brochures full of descriptions and photographs of all the chicks they supplied. Glancing through it, Wee Daft Dicky, though better informed, was none the wiser. Eventually, after much head-scratching, he settled on two kinds; Rhode Island Red, which he noted down as, 'Road Dining Red' because red was his favourite colour and Cinnamon Queen, which he noted down as China-man Queen. After all, he thought, it would taste good at Christmas.

His mind firmly set on two breeds of chicken, the man he knew, who knew a man, asked the obvious question,

"How many do you want Dicky?"

Dithering, Wee Daft Dicky chewing on a fingernail answered, "One or two."

"Hundred?"

"Auch, catch yourself on, man. What would I do with one or two hundred chickens?"

"Dozen then?"

"No. Look, I only want one or two. That's all," he said, gesturing with fingers for emphasis. For a moment, the man misinterpreted the gesture. They stood, the pair of them looking at each other, their misunderstanding evaporating like morning mist before the rising sun.

"I might be able to get you half a dozen," the man he knew, who knew a man, begrudgingly offered.

"But, but…"

"No buts Dicky. That's it, take or leave it," the man he knew said, turning and walking away.

The following Saturday morning, Wee Daft Dicky's mother answered a knock on the door. The man Dicky knew was standing with what his mother thought was a box of pastries under his arm.

"Richaaaaaard," she yelled, "there's a man here at the door with a box of pastries for you."

Wee Daft Dicky rushed to the door, stepped outside, closed it, keeping his mother inside, out of earshot. "Sorry, I don't want her to know what I'm planning," he told the man he knew.

"I've got you four that were leftover from another order. It was the best I could do."

"But, but…"

"No buts Dicky. Take or leave it. It's up to you. If you don't want them, someone else will."

"OK, I'll take them."

"You'll have to look after them well for the first week or two. They're only three days old, not long out of the incubator. Ok?"

"What?" Dicky queried, displaying his lack of knowledge of chicken farming.

"You'll have to keep them warm, fed and watered for a couple of weeks."

"Right," Dicky said, suggesting he knew all that.

"Have you a place ready for them then?"

"I have," Dicky assured the man he knew who knew some-body…

But Wee Daft Dicky didn't have a place prepared for the chicks, sitting huddled together like candy floss in their white cardboard box.

Inside, avoiding his mother, he hurried upstairs to his bed-room, desperately trying to figure out what to do with his four chicks. Wee Daft Dicky stashed the box in his wardrobe, cov-ered with a blanket to keep the chicks warm. Satisfied, he headed downstairs to face the maternal inquisition. At the bottom of the stairs, he paused, turned and rushed back to his bedroom to re-move the blanket covering the box. Just in time, he realised that the chicks needed air. Only then, with the blanket removed, did he see the air holes in the sides of the box.

Relieved, Dicky, disaster averted, returned to the lion's den to face interrogation. His foot had barely cleared the last tread on the stairs when he heard his mother's summons.

"Richaaaard!"

"Yes, Mother," he obediently responded to her beckoning.

"What did that man want with you, Richard?"

Wee Daft Dicky, quick on his feet, spun his mother a yarn about getting an electric light put into the lavatory for her and roofing the yard with Perspex to keep her from getting wet when it rained, and she needed to go to the toilet.

"That's a lot, Richard, to fit into a wee box."

"All that's in the box, Mother, is bits of paper, ideas of what's needed so that the work can be costed."

Sitting up as close to the fire as she could, his mother chit-tered on. Dicky, sitting opposite on a straight-backed, uncomfortable wooden chair, thought that if her toes were any closer to the grate, Ashie-pelt* would be an apt descriptor. Without pausing for breath, she chattered on, her legs spread wide to capture as much heat as she could under her patchwork woollen skirt, which had seen better days. Dicky's eyes rested on the cavernous heated space behind his mother's knees under the chaise lounge. He had found a safe, warm, cosy hideaway for his chicks.

With his mother in bed for her afternoon rest, Dicky fetched his box of chicks downstairs and carefully placed them out of sight under the fainting couch as his mother called the chaise lounge. Lifting the box lid to have a wee peep, he saw his chicks huddled together like little balls of yellow fluff in the corner. He placed a shallow dish filled with water in the opposite corner with a feed tray of bread crumbs and assorted seeds beside it. Quietly closing the box, he left the chicks to themselves.

Everything was proceeding according to plan, if Dicky had one, until arriving home tired after a hard day looking for work, his mother greeted him.

"Richard, I think there's a mouse in this house. I saw it sitting there, gawking up at me as if it owned the place. I hit it a swipe with my fly swatter, but I don't know where it went. See if you can see any sign of it. You know I won't sleep the night with a mouse in the house."

Dicky looked all around the room and found nothing. He searched the scullery, too, but there was no sign of a mouse. *No mouse with any sense would come in here,* Dicky was thinking as he searched. Believing his mother was seeing things, he got down on his knees to have a look under the fainting couch. He found it. It was dead. But it wasn't a mouse. It was one of his little fluffy chicks. He gathered it up in his hands and, rising through clenched teeth, said, "You got it, Mother. You got the mouse, alright. I'll bin it now. You'll be able to sleep tonight. No worries."

He didn't bin it. Dicky buried the chick out the back in Magill's field, marking the spot with a round white stone. The most active of his chicks, it had somehow gotten out of the box and fallen foul of his mother's fly swatter. He rehoused the chicks in a bigger, deeper cardboard box at the first opportunity.

His mother's eyesight wasn't the best, but she could hear a pin drop when it suited her, and so keen was her nose she could tell who was passing the front door by the smell of their sweaty feet. She, as folk would say, was every inch a super smeller.

Sitting opposite his mother one evening, who was as close to the fire as she could get without being in it, reading his paper, she looked over at him and snapped, " Richard, your socks need changing. I can smell them from here."

"Yes, Mother, I will in a minute."

Dicky, slyly sniffing a few times, couldn't detect any lingering odours. He didn't have his mother's acute sense of smell but knew it wasn't his socks she was whiffing. The only thing he could think she was smelling was the chickens in the box underneath where she was sitting. "Couldn't be, he told himself. Sure, I thoroughly cleaned their box this morning."

"There's been a funny smell about the house these past few days. Are you changing clothes often enough? Is it something you're working with or what?"

That night, his mother safely in bed, Dicky got down on his knees as if in prayer at the side of the fainting couch. Easing the chicken box out, he lifted the lid and lowered his head inside it, sniffing in search of the offending smell. He found it. The faintest whiff of ammonia negotiated its way up his nostrils, forcing him to jerk his head back, banging it severely against the substantial frame of the longue. Putting everything back in its place, Dicky knew his mother wouldn't cease. He would have to do something very soon.

The next day, his mother collared him again.

"Richard, do you hear anything?"

He wanted to say, only your voice, mother but resisted the temptation. "No, not a thing, Mother."

"You must be hard of hearing. Come over here a minute and listen."

Dicky hearing the chicks cheeping contentedly, tried to divert his mother's attention.

"I hear something right enough. You've got great ears, Mother. Big Tam next door has moved his chiming clock over against the other side of the party wall. It's only half-a-brick thick, you know."

"Well, it's some clock, alright, for it's been chiming every second, day and night. It never stops. You'll have to do something about it, Richard."

"I will, Mother. I'll have a word with him. It'll be all right. Big Tam's okay."

Dicky had been hard at work readying the shed to receive the chicks. The prescient moment had arrived. That evening Dicky moved the chicks into their new home. They had more floor space to exercise, and roosts on the shed walls to rest on. Closing the shed door, he secured it with a padlock.

The chicks were growing fast. They'd be pullets soon, not that Dicky knew a pullet from a cockerel. They needed more space to exercise and grow. He let them out into the narrow yard without his mother seeing them. His routine was to feed and water the chicks early in the morning and let them have the freedom of the yard for a while before his mother left her bed. The procedure was repeated afternoons and evenings when his mother was resting.

The pigeon racing season was in full swing. Mornings and evenings, the sky overhead was filled with flocks of swirling, swooshing pigeons exercising, some flying so low their wings were heard clapping together. Dicky's birds down in the narrow yard saw and heard them. Had Dicky been attentive, he would have noticed his birds cocking their beady eyes upwards. Encouraged by what they saw overhead, the chickens ran up and down the yard, stretching their legs and flapping their wings. They were learning to fly. Dicky's birds were testing their growing flight feathers. One feather was the same as another to Dicky. It never crossed Dicky's mind to pick up the birds, spread their wings the way a pigeon fancier would and examine them. In a few days, the chickens were flying the length of the yard. Unaware that chickens could fly distances of thirty yards or more at heights of two or three yards above the ground, Dicky left their flight feathers untrimmed.

As usual, one morning Dicky fed the chickens, let them out into the yard to exercise and went into the scullery to fetch fresh water. Suddenly, the chickens began madly squawking. Rushing out, thinking they'd wake his mother, he saw a big black, green-eyed cat with a chicken's neck in its mouth glaring defiantly at him. Horrified, he dropped the water, grabbed the yard brush, and ran to rescue his chicken. He swung at the cat with the brush, but it was too quick and agile. Chicken by the neck, it scrambled up the yard door, ran across the wall and disappeared out of sight. Dicky went out the yard door like a shot from a gun raced up the Bacs, frantically pursuing it, but it was gone.

Anxiously haring up and down the Bac's, he desperately searched for any sign of his poor wee chicken, a feather, anything. There was nothing. He climbed the steps to every pigeon loft on the Brae and, scanning all around, saw nothing. At his wit's end, he fetched his ladder, pitched it against his neighbour's walls and looked into their backyards. Neighbours alerted to what had happened joined in the search. But it was all in vain.

The cat and his chicken were gone, vanished. The big black cat, it seemed, was an outsider. It didn't belong to anyone on the Brae. The pigeon men could have taught Dicky a thing or two about cats and birds. But as always, Wee Daft Dicky had to learn the hard way.

Dicky now had two chickens; the Rhode Island Red and the Cinnamon Queen. Inevitably the morning dawned when Dicky's mother left her bed unexpectantly early, raising the window blind to discover the two chickens in her backyard.

"Richaaaaaard! Birds are flapping about in our yard. What are they doing there?"

"They're a couple of pigeons, mother, that got lost on their way home in the race, I think. I'm trying to find out who they belong to."

"And how are you going to do that?"

"The pigeon men will find out who they belong to from the rings on their legs. Don't you worry, Mother; once they're fit and strong, they'll be on their way back home."

"Make sure. I don't want pigeons under my feet when I'm hanging out washing."

"I'll make a place for them in the shed for a day or two. Alright?"

It would have been alright if Dicky had cut the chicken's flight feathers. But he hadn't, and his birds, thinking they were pigeons, wanted to join the flocking flights above them. Weeks passed, and the chickens, full-flight feathered, flew up and down the narrow yard with eyes cocked on the skies above.

The final pigeon race of the season was on the last Saturday in September. Groups of men stood around on street corners to hear if - *the birds were up yet* - meaning, in layman's terms, waiting to hear if the pigeons had been released in Skibbereen, all the way down in County Cork, to race home. The release confirmed, the men returned to their lofts to begin the long hopeful vigil that might joyfully end with their pigeon clocking the best time.

Dicky was not at home that morning, but knowing it was race day had his chickens safely housed in the shed. He had forgotten to fill the coal bucket and lock the shed door in his haste. As the morning wore on, the fire burned close to extinction, forcing Dicky's mother to tend to the fire herself. She wasn't best pleased when she saw the coal bucket was empty. Muttering, rehearsing what she would say to Richard when he returned, she made her way in lousy humour to the shed. When she opened the door, the chickens, squawking, flew out, scaring the daylights out of her. They flew up and down the yard past her, squawking louder and louder as they went.

Gathering herself together, she thought, I'll teach them a lesson and, grabbing a mop, ran up and down the yard, flailing at them with all her might. The terrified chickens did what came naturally; they took flight. First, onto the ladder Dicky had set against the wall and then onto the yard wall. The failing mop made them fly up the Bacs, alerting neighbours as they went. From the walls of the backyards, the chickens flew across and settled on a pigeon loft.

Everybody was out the Bacs watching the commotion. The chickens, the centre of attention, enjoying their newfound freedom, flew zigzagging to and fro up and down the Bacs from pigeon loft to pigeon loft and the backyard walls. They were having a ball doing an aerial version of the chicken dance routine.

The pigeon men weren't best pleased. The race was on; nothing could stop it, but no racing pigeon would access its home loft with the commotion up and down the Bacs and around the pigeon lofts. Big Tam, Dicky's neighbour, appeared with his solution to the problem. He was raising his double-barrelled shotgun to his shoulder when Wee Daft Dicky appeared on the scene and, on bended knees, pleaded for the lives of his chickens.

"Let me try?" He begged, "They know me."

"You have an hour, Dicky. That's it."

Dicky tried talking to the chickens. They weren't listening. He tried tempting them with barley and corn. They ignored his offering.

Up the Bacs, wee Lizzie Earl was bringing in her washing from a line strung across the right-of-way. Her hearing wasn't that good, but she was surprised to see a couple of pigeons flying around on race day morning.

Meanwhile Dicky, with a fisherman's net on the end of a long pole, chased the chickens up the Bacs towards Lizzie. Her washing line was strung across the chicken's flight path, trying to reach a pigeon loft beyond it. They had to go over, under or around it. It was chicken make-up your mind time. Lizzie, arms up, stretching to unpin a sheet, hidden from the chicken's line of sight, was unaware that the heavier of the two birds, the Rhode Island Red, was heading straight for her like an overladen jumbo jet. The backyard wall was higher than Lizzie's clothesline. The Rhode Island Red leapt off, lost elevation, and, unable to regain it, ploughed into the sheet, knocking Lizzie flat on her back.

Fortunately, Lizzie, although winded, wasn't seriously injured. Dicky, racing up, captured the Rhode Island Red before it escaped from Lizzie's sheet. The white Cinnamon Queen disappeared over the brow of the Brae and was last seen entering a thicket at the far end of Hunter's field. Excitement abated; a quiet, tense expectation filled the afternoon as eyes up and down the Brae searched the sky for homing pigeons.

The Rhode Island Red chick had grown into a lovely meaty bird that would sit well on any Christmas table. Dicky bless his heart, had grown fond of it. His dilemma was twofold; he didn't know how to despatch it humanely, and he didn't know how to prepare it for roasting. He thought the chickens hung up in the butcher's shops looked great, regretting that he'd decided to rear his own. Panic-stricken, he went next door and, explaining his predicament, asked Big Tam to shoot it with his double-barrelled gun. Big Tam laughed.

"Dicky, if I do that, they'll have me up for murder."

"What are you talking about?"

"If I shoot it and your mother eats it, she'll die of lead poisoning, and I'll get the blame."

"Oh. What's the best way to do it then?"

"It's up to you. There's the broomstick method, the wooden block and axe method and the neck stretching method. Your choice Dicky." Seeing that Dicky's heart wasn't in it and he hadn't the stomach for it, Big Tam said, "Look, bring it around a few days before Christmas, and I'll do it for you. OK?"

"Great. Thank you."

"It'll give you time to get it ready for roasting on the big day."

"Get it ready?"

"Aye, gut it and pluck it."

"Right."

But Big Tam saw through Dicky. "You have to clean out its intestines."

"It's what?"

"The heart, liver, lungs and all."

"Right."

"And you have to make sure its cavity is clean."

"It's ready for the roasting then?"

"After you've plucked it."

"Plucked it?"

"Dicky, you can't roast the chicken with the feathers still on it. Can you?"

"No, I wouldn't think you could."

Parting, Big Tam was convinced Wee Daft Dicky hadn't a clue about preparing his chicken for roasting.

On the morning of the 24th of December, Wee Daft Dicky called at Big Tam's to collect his slain bird. He wasn't looking forward to receiving the dead bird but, having set out on the journey, was determined to see it through to the end. The thought of the gutting and plucking didn't fill him with joy. But needs must, as they say.

Big Tam ushered Dicky into the house, sat him down, fetched another cup from the scullery and poured him some tea. They could hear the sound of Mary, Big Tam's wife, working in the scullery.

"Are you nearly done in there, Mary, Dicky's here for his chicken."

"Another five minutes is all I need."

"Five minutes Dicky and you'll have your chicken."

From the grunts and groans from the kitchen, Dicky wondered if Mary was killing the chicken herself. Then the noises stopped. All was quiet. A few moments passed before Mary emerged from the scullery, proudly holding the plucked, gutted chicken up by its legs in front of her stained apron, like a trophy. She held a parcel of her homemade stuffing in her other hand.

Wee Daft Dicky didn't know what to say, relieved he hadn't to pluck and gut his chicken he was also delighted to see how meaty his hand-reared chicken looked. He left Big Tam's with Mary's instructions on how to roast the chicken, and lest he forget, she'd written them down for him.

Christmas lunch with his mother was more than better than last year's; it was the best ever. His mother complimented Dicky on everything, including the stuffing, remarking that it tasted better than Mary's next door. Dicky passed no remarks.

Some years later, Big Tam collared Wee Daft Dicky, took him aside, saying, "Do you mind that party up the Brae?"

"What party?"

"Mrs Carson's party*."

"That was a while ago."

"Never mind that. I've something here to show you," Big Tam said, passing Dicky a sheet of paper with a poem on it entitled Mrs Carson's Party.

Dicky concentrated his mind on reading.

For large and small. For one and all,
I've got exciting news,
My news is not bad, just a party we had,
The Rolls-Royces' were lined up in queues.

This town of renown, at the head of the town,
Is sure to be mentioned in history,
How the house was filled, without any being killed,
To me is an absolute mystery.

The rowdies from Larne made the parlour a barn,
Mrs Carson went wrong in the head,
The time that she had drove the poor woman mad,
through the ceiling came the leg of the bed.

Now, this was not all, in fact, it was small,
By the thing that occurred after dark,

More trouble began, Rab Shields killed a hen,
And everyone rushed to the park.

Wee Daft Dicky stopped reading, raised his head and, looking at Big Tam, said, "Do you think it was a white one?"

"I wouldn't be surprised. Sure, you know what he's like."

Rab Shields lived a few doors above Dicky. He didn't keep pigeons but was known to be partial to a nice bit of chicken.

Notes:

Ashie-pelt: An Ulster word meaning someone sitting by the fire with their toes in the grate.

Mrs Carson's Party: This poem was first published in *The Corran* - A Larne and District Folklore Society magazine. The author is unknown.

Acknowledgements

Thank you to my friend and mentor, Eileen Watt, for nurturing me on this journey of discovery with incredible fortitude.

I am forever indebted to Margaret Stewart for her generous and emboldening words of encouragement.

Rev Father Joseph Rooney, thank you for your kind assistance. Your information is the foundation for the 'What's In a Name' story.

The poem 'Children' appeared earlier in my book *Naked Windows* (2020).

Annette, who has read every word, including rewrites, of which there were many, I am eternally grateful.

About the cover

The covers for *A Cairndhu Nightingale and Other Tales,* which bring to mind Cairndhu House, the former residence of Sir Thomas and Lady Edith Dixon and the glory of its gardens when it was a convalescent hospital, are from Northern Irish artist Cherie Craig's original paintings. Cherie, raised in Larne, read the story and, searching for its soul, found it.

An extract from Scene through a Rearview Mirror

She was home alone when she felt the needle-sharp pain searing her side. Her hand, as if it had a mind of its own, pressed hard against her skin to ease it, but it was not for easing, just like the stitch she sometimes endured when jogging, but much more intense. She gritted her teeth, hoping it would pass, and continued with what she was doing. She was hanging out the washing, lifting a heavy blanket and stretching to lob it over the clothesline, when an excruciating stab of pain brought her crumbling to her knees. Gasping, she knelt on the grass, tears in her eyes, unable to move, helpless. Eventually willing herself to move, she gathered up the wet blanket, made her way crab-like back into the house, and collapsed onto the floor.

An extract from *Naked Windows*

It was a rough crossing. The mutinous black seas lashed the
boat, relentlessly tossing it about like a cork in a turbulent
stream. Sitting alone in a black-and-white habit, the Cross and
Pasion nun furiously fingered her beads. The head-on wind increased to gale force, and mountainous waves played with the
boat, hurling it around like an orca toying with a doomed seal.
Beleaguered, the nun clung to the railing, thankful her stomach
was empty. Clutching her rosary beads, she prayed the sorrowful
mysteries: the Agony in the Garden, the Scourging at the Pillar,
the Crowning with Thorns, the Carrying of the Cross, and the
Crucifixion. In her desperation, she wasn't praying. She was petitioning her Lord of the Cross to rescue her from drowning,
like a child pleading for a good exam grade.

Sister Clare couldn't swim.

An extract from Seasons of Affection

There had been no rain for several days; the ground was firm,
crawling slowly, stealthily, noiselessly towards the window near-
est the Major, out of sight through the shrubbery, until he was
within hearing distance. In position, he froze, scarcely breathing,
melting into the shrubbery. Listening to the discussion his pulse
rate increased until his heart pounded his ribcage. It wasn't op-
position; it was insurrection. Delivery of vast quantities of arms
already procured, as scheduled and confirmed, was greeted with
apostolic applause.

About the Author

Jim shields was born on the Mill brae, Larne, Northern Ireland in 1943. His schooling began in the Mc Kenna Memorial Primary School and continued in Larne Technical College. On completion of his apprenticeship in the construction industry he pursued further education, taking night classes to obtain professional and academic accreditations.

He completed his MSc in Fire Safety Engineering at the University of Edinburgh, followed by his PhD in the same discipline at The University of Ulster.

Jim, Emeritus Professor of Fire Safety Engineering, retired from his academic career in 2004.

A passionate supporter of the arts he was a relative latecomer to creative writing, but once started he has striven to make up for lost time. is his third published collection of short stories. He has no intention of it being his last.

Other works by Jim:
Scene through a Rearview Mirror – 2019
Naked Widows – 2020
Seasons of Affection – 2022

Jim and his wife Annette still live in Larne where they regularly entertain their children and grandchildren.

9 781923 020573